THE AWAY TEAM

Illustrated by Trevor Parkin

D1493860

The Away Team

Michael Hardcastle

MAMMOTH

First published in Great Britain 1992
by Methuen Children's Books Ltd
Published 1993 by Mammoth
an imprint of Reed International Books Ltd
Michelin House, 81 Fulham Road, London SW3 6RB
and Auckland, Melbourne, Singapore and Toronto

Reprinted 1993, 1994, 1995, 1996

ISBN 0 7497 0962 6

A CIP catalogue record for this title
is available from the British Library

Printed and bound in Great Britain
by Cox & Wyman Ltd, Reading, Berkshire

Contents

ONE

Leaving Home

'Listen,' Damian said fiercely as his team was about to return to the pitch for the second half of the Sunday League match against Kettlesing. 'We can't lose our last home game at the Fold. It'd never be forgotten, it'd be the worst thing possible. So we've got to go out there and get stuck into that lot – and WIN. Nothing else will do. OK?'

Most of the other Darton United players nodded or murmured something to show they agreed with their captain. Normally, Damian's manner was mild and it was almost unheard of for him to shout at his players except in the heat of a moment during a match. But then this was a day full of emotions and so no one was surprised that Damian should feel so strongly about the result of what otherwise would have been a fairly ordinary League match.

'Stevie, something I want to tell you,' Damian called as the speedy winger was about to break into a fast sprint. Obediently, Stevie turned and trotted back towards him. 'I want you to run at their defence this half, not hold back like you have been doing. You've got the pace and you've got a good shot, so use 'em. You haven't even started to get into this game yet.'

Stevie's brown eyes blinked. 'Actually, I'm lucky I haven't got a broken leg or something. That big full-back with all the black hair has been trying to kick a hole through me every time I've been anywhere near him. But the ref doesn't seem to see anything he does.'

'Well, just kick him back next time he tries something. Maybe that'll sort him out. Just don't let him get away with it. We won't win if we're a lot of cowards.'

Once again, Stevie blinked, surprised at Damian's tone. He was as keen to win the match as anyone and he thought the skipper would have recognised the effort he was making to outwit Kettlesing's defence. Normally his pace was enough to keep him clear of trouble but the player marking him was every bit as fast as he was.

As he lined up in his customary place on the left side of midfield, Damian wondered whether he'd been too harsh. Stevie, always modest in spite of his talents as a player, invariably responded to praise, so had Damian undermined his confidence by criticising him so strongly and not being sympathetic to Stevie's problems with the violent full-back? Possibly. On the other hand, most of the team were in a wimpish mood this morning; in the skipper's view, a rocket fired off here and there might make them realise what was needed. Perhaps he'd become too soft with them, perhaps they were taking him for granted in his third season as United's captain. Perhaps, he now told himself, he should set an example: instead of sticking to his role as a prompter and provider he could move up and try to seize a scoring opportunity for himself.

Because of their name, Kettlesing were the subject of plenty of puns and jokes, especially ones about their being 'steamed up' or 'on the boil', and they were often known as the Whistlers. There was no doubt that they were on song against Darton and the goal by which they led at half-time was really much less than they deserved. Twice within a minute Hajinder, United's wonderfully agile goalkeeper, had foiled their attack with point-blank saves when a goal had appeared a certainty, and on two more occasions their forwards had missed the easiest of scoring chances through over-eagerness and the desire to smash the ball into the net rather than place it beyond the goalie's reach.

Damian expected them to resume where they'd left off, eager to consolidate their lead with at least one more goal. But if United could pin them back immediately by launching their own attacks and getting the equalizer perhaps Kettlesing would panic and start to crumble. He had to hope it would work out that way. At this early stage of the season, both teams were anxious for points that would underline their promotion prospects, especially as they'd only narrowly missed going up the previous season. A victory today over close rivals would be a double fillip.

'Mine!' Damian yelled and charged towards Neil Dallimore, United's gangling striker, who had possession of the ball but seemed to be living up to his nickname of Dalli-a-lot. Although plainly startled by his captain's command Neil managed to transfer the ball to him and Damian, swerving easily past the first opponent to come at him, surged away towards the right flank, always a favourite area of his when he wanted to set something up. Stevie was out on the touchline, his marker in close attendance as usual. As he headed towards the touchline Damian signalled by cupping his right hand and repeatedly jerking it towards his chest that he wanted the winger to run towards him. What Damian had in mind was a quick one-two pass that would allow him to move into space well ahead of Stevie's marker.

Even though Damian and some of his team-mates had used this ploy before Stevie was slow to respond, almost as if he simply didn't understand what was expected. In fact, he was both worried by the proximity of his marker and still resentful of Damian's criticism. By the time he'd made up his mind to move and take the ball it was too late for the ploy to work. Almost in the same moment that Damian flicked the ball to him Stevie was sent crashing to the ground by a scything tackle from the full-back, who had guessed what was going to happen next.

Stevie was writhing in pain and rolling over and

over as the referee blew a powerful blast on his whistle and summoned the offender to stand before him. Plainly exasperated by the missed chance to make significant progress towards the Kettlesing penalty area, Damian nonetheless went across to ascertain the extent of his team-mate's injury – if, indeed, he really was injured.

'Come on, it's not as bad as all that,' he murmured, bending down to touch Stevie on the shoulder. 'And the guy who did you's getting the yellow card.'

'About time,' Stevie muttered, which proved to Damian that the suffering was more in the mind than in the body. But when Stevie at last got to his feet and rolled down his left sock his captain was taken aback to see an ugly red mark and scratches on the calf just behind the area covered by the shin pad. 'That's where he got me last time. So I expect I'll have a worse bruise now.'

He limped away as Warren Snowball, United's other midfield forager, lined up the free kick in consultation with Damian. The skipper himself decided to go into the box. In spite of his own lack of height, he could jump practically as high as Neil when necessary, an attribute that sometimes took defences by surprise. So far he hadn't ventured far upfield in this match but now might be the time to do so. United needed a goal at this stage to provide a springboard to victory.

'Head it right back across the box to me,' Damian instructed Neil softly as he ran past him to station himself by the far post. Neil, who'd seemed to shoot up in recent months, was easily the tallest player on the pitch. Now was the ideal opportunity to use his great height to the best advantage, just so long as Warren found him with the free kick.

Automatically Neil moved towards the near post, taking a couple of worried defenders with him, and because he deliberately kept shifting his position as he awaited the ball they were getting in each other's way. Warren floated the ball in with great precision and, after needing to take only one stride, Neil rose like a salmon to meet it. Unhappily, though he got direction into his header, he failed to get power and the ball wasn't going to reach its target.

Realising it was going to fall short of him, Damian made a desperate dive to try to reach it before anyone else could clear it. He was within centimetres of making contact with the ball when, without even seeing the obstacle, he stumbled and fell heavily over a defender's outstretched leg, winding himself as he crashed to the ground.

Coolly, and with an economy of effort that Haji could admire, the Kettlesing goalkeeper darted from his line, grabbed the ball as it bounced invitingly in front of him, advanced to the eighteen-yard line and hurled it to his own skipper. He in turn wasted no time either before hitting a pass to the centre-forward, loitering just over the halfway line. With United's defence having pushed up in support of Warren's free kick, the Kettlesing striker had what he saw as an ocean of space ahead of him. Head

down and over the ball, he raced away from the two Darton players who gave chase.

Haji came out to meet him. He really had no option because if he remained on his line the attacker would have the entire width of the net to aim at; so all the goalie could do was narrow the angle for the shot and hope to put him off his aim. He wasn't successful. The striker bent to go one way, turned the other, and with good skill steered the ball round Haji before sliding it comfortably into the back of the net.

In its simplicity, it was the classic breakaway goal.

Damian, still rubbing his stomach and wheezing a little, watched events from the opposite penalty area. And when the ball entered the net he sank to his knees again momentarily, utterly deflated. Another goal for Kettlesing was just what he'd wanted to avoid.It seemed to him his world was crumbling about him. His team was playing like a group of strangers who've only just met and haven't a clue what each of the others is capable of doing. On this form, they hadn't the remotest hope of gaining promotion. Lying heavily on top of everything was the black cloud of homelessness: after this match, Darton United wouldn't have a football ground of their own. Every match would have to be played on a borrowed pitch or at the home of their opponents.

The discomfort of his full-length fall began to recede, and Damian hurried back to his own half of the pitch. There was no point in castigating anybody for the second goal: no United player had really been at fault. Kettlesing had glimpsed a chance to increase their lead and had taken it brilliantly.

'Come on, boys, we can still win this one,' he called loudly to rally his players. 'We've come from two-down before. Let's do it again.'

He meant every word. A team leading by two goals was often inclined to relax a little, thinking they'd done enough, whereas they continued to fight tigerishly when they were only one up. In Damian's view 0-3 was the truly crushing scoreline; you hadn't a lot of hope of overcoming that, particularly if time was against you.

'Warren, keep possession, go at 'em, go *forward*,' he urged the long-legged, grey-eyed boy with the perpetually calm manner. Some people had suggested that Warren didn't have enough passion to win anything but Damian thought differently. He had great faith in Warren's talent and determination to succeed when he had an objective in mind.

Warren, who never said much at any time about anything, just nodded. He'd scored a number of goals for United but never wanted to play as an out-and-out striker: he preferred, he'd once told Damian, to create chances for others to take. In an emergency, though, he was usually prepared to change his role in the team. And Damian now considered they were in that emergency.

As he'd hoped they would, several Kettlesing players visibly relaxed now that their side had the cushion of a two-goal advantage. So it wasn't surprising that they backed off when Warren began to run at them, expecting, anyway, that he would part with the ball quickly. He didn't. With sudden acceleration, he took the opposite route to Damian's, curving away towards the left wing; that didn't seem to defenders to offer much of a threat and they let him go. Naturally, however, the goalkeeper drifted to that side of his penalty area, almost as if he simply wanted to have a better view of what might be happening near the touchline. It certainly never occurred to him that the leggy midfielder with the ball at his toes was hoping to entice him out of position.

Without appearing even to look up, let alone assess any distances, Warren swung his left foot and drove the ball hard and high into the centre of the box. The goalie was dreadfully slow to realise what was happening. For a moment or two he thought he might be able to turn and run and catch the ball, but then he saw that was impossible. All he could do was to jump and divert it for a corner. That idea didn't work either. His fingers just touched the ball as it went by, and that contact was sufficient to change its direction by a fraction into the path of the in-rushing Neil Dallimore. Even Dalli-a-lot in his most careless mood didn't miss such gifts as this one. The distraught goalie was still trying to recover his balance as the ball bulged the net.

'Great cross, great RUN, Icy,' Damian cried, rushing across to embrace the goal creator and using the only nickname Warren would tolerate. 'Now we need another – and then . . .'

'Never stood a chance, that goalie!' chortled Neil, looking round for further congratulatons. 'Saw that cross coming up a mile away, that's why I was dead on target, as usual.'

That remark, at least, was nonsense but nobody said so; his team-mates were well used to Neil's extravagant self-praise after scoring an ordinary sort of goal. But it helped his self-confidence and that was what mattered.

'I'll get the next one,' vowed Danny Clixby, United's newest recruit, a small, combative forward with dark, spiky hair.

Damian nodded his approval and glanced up at his favourite, sometimes inspiring view: Bowler Hill, its right-hand slope surmounted by three distinctive trees. The hill had nothing to do with cricket, having been named, someone once told him, after the hat. The trio of trees, however, reminded him of cricket stumps – or, even more appropriately, a hat-trick. For the umpteenth time in recent weeks it crossed his mind that it was a view he wouldn't be seeing again from the centre of United's home pitch. All too soon the ground would be covered with new houses and United would be homeless. So they *had* to get something out of this final match at the Fold.

His concentration returned to the game. Just as he'd supposed, Kettlesing were distinctly jittery following that goal 'from out of the blue', as they saw it. Their skipper had been furious with the

17

goalkeeper and he, in turn, had laid into the defenders who should have been covering him.

Trying to make up for their defence's lapse, the Kettlesing forwards launched an immediate counter-attack but in their over-eagerness to consolidate their lead they merely got in each other's way. Alex Anson, Darton's two-footed left-back, made a neat interception. Riding a clumsy tackle, he carried the ball upfield, dummied his way past a bemused opponent, and then swung the ball across to Stevie Pailthorp.

Cleverly, Stevie didn't try to bring the ball under control. Instead, allowing it to bounce once, he hammered it towards Neil who was lurking on the edge of the penalty area.

'Neil, Neil!' Danny yelled at him, desperate for a pass. In spite of the fact that he himself was being closely marked, the big striker ignored the call. Trying to pull the ball down and get off a shot in the same movement, he succeeded only in ballooning it high over the bar. It was an appalling effort and Danny told him so in strong terms.

'There was nobody near me, I couldn't have missed,' Danny added bitterly.

Damian agreed with him but there was no point in saying anything further to Neil, who at least looked ashamed of his effort. They'd just have to start again.

Understandably, but unwisely, Kettlesing tried to play it safe, thinking there wasn't much time left in this match. In Damian's view there was quite enough time for Darton to score two goals and win. He began to urge his players on again, issuing instructions in quick-fire fashion. He'd read somewhere that a team that communicates is in command, a phrase he rather relished. So, this season, the United players had been encouraged to call and talk to each other, not only to help a team-mate but also to unsettle the opposition. So far as the skipper could tell, the tactic was paying off. He had the firm impression that conversation added confidence.

'Yours!' he called, sliding the ball across to Stevie, hovering again near the touchline with his shadow in attendance as usual. This time, however, the Darton winger brought off a trick that completely outwitted his opponent. Recently, on television, he'd seen it performed by an international player and Stevie suddenly remembered he wanted to do it, too. Instead of trapping the ball, he back-heeled it and, in the same fluid movement, spun round to retrieve it. His marker, moving in from the side, was left floundering.

Thrilled by the success of his manoeuvre, the pacey No. 7 shot clear of everyone as he ran wide towards the dead-ball line. Although he'd scored some good goals in past seasons he'd no intention of trying to finish off this movement on his own. Both Neil and Danny were arrowing towards the box, eager for a pass. Kettlesing expected that the ball would go to the towering centre-forward to try a header. But they were utterly wrong – Stevie hadn't forgotten how Neil had wasted the last pass.

'Yours, Dan!' he yelled, and hit a fierce, low cross towards his smaller team-mate. Confident and capable of taking any pass, however awkwardly it might reach him, Danny turned to meet the ball and pull it under control. He was just about to transfer it to his left foot for a snap shot when a defender, desperate to get hold of the ball, knocked him flat.

'PENALTY!' roared several voices, including Damian's. From where he was, it looked a blatant foul. Plainly it was because the referee didn't hesitate before pointing to the penalty spot. 'Yes!' Damian exclaimed immediately, feeling as if his prayers had been answered.

But, just as swiftly, doubts clouded his mind. Who should be entrusted with the kick?

Danny, always desperate to get amongst the goals in any circumstances, hadn't risen to his feet yet: both the referee and some of the Kettlesing players were showing some concern about a possible injury. Ironically, the eager Danny was always ready to appeal for a penalty kick whenever he was so much as brushed against in the box. Haji, who had his own views on penalty kicks, naturally enough, had dubbed his team-mate 'Danny the Diver', and it wasn't unfair. Danny, though, hadn't dived this time and he had seemed about to score. Even if he'd only been shaken by his fall he wouldn't be calm enough to take the spot kick, Damian reflected.

Warren Snowball possessed the most accurate shot of all the United players, but Damian also believed that the midfielder with the cool, grey eyes wouldn't enjoy the responsibility of taking this kick. Warren was really a loner, someone who reacted spontaneously and, often, surprisingly; he didn't always calculate the possible consequences. Damian glanced in his direction and saw that, even at this moment, Warren had his head down and his back towards goal, apparently in his own world.

Danny at last accepted the ref's hand and was pulled to his feet and then, anguish written all over his face, he began to hobble around in a rather theatrical way as if to show how badly he was suffering. With no bones broken, no wounds in the flesh and a penalty kick already awarded, it was hardly necessary. But Danny was simply being Danny.

Purposefully, Damian strode towards the twelve-yard spot, picking up the ball on the way and rubbing it clean against his apple-green shirt. If United failed to score, if they failed to get the vital equalizer, then he could blame only himself. It was a captain's responsibility to take a penalty kick as important as this one. If he scored, it would be a moment to remember. *If? When* I score, he told himself.

Kettlesing's goalkeeper, he'd noted, wasn't very big: in fact, hardly any taller than Hajinder. So Damian would aim for the top of the net, the top corner to the goalie's left if possible. If he could find the angle then it would be almost impossible for the boy in the red shirt to reach the ball.

'Good luck!' Alex called as Damian ran in. Luck, though, wasn't needed. With his left foot, Damian struck the ball cleanly, accurately and powerfully – and it soared to its target like a guided missile. Even though he managed a despairing leap the goalie wasn't within a metre of the ball as it lifted the netting.

'Great, great, great!' Damian exulted as teammates rushed to embrace him. They were going to get a point out of this match after all; and he still believed there was time for United to grab the winner.

There wasn't. Despite frantic efforts to mount more attacks, the home side couldn't make the necessary breakthrough again. So the penalty was the very last goal scored at the Fold.

'Could've been worse,' Alex Anson remarked to his captain as they trooped off the pitch. 'I mean, we could easily have lost that game the way we were playing.'

'I agree,' nodded Damian, trying to keep his mind off other matters. 'We showed spirit at the end, we came back from the dead. That's progress. That's good news.'

The bad news, he was soon to discover, was awaiting him at home.

TWO

Injury Time

Even as he walked down the street he could see that his mother's silver saloon was not parked in its usual place – which was very odd. Sue Tennant was precise and organized in everything she did, which was just as well for someone with a social life as hectic as hers. That morning she'd been playing one of her regular badminton partners and Damian was faintly surprised she was home before he was. Perhaps, he speculated before opening the front door, she'd won so easily they'd returned home for an early lunch; or maybe her opponent simply hadn't turned up and his mum hadn't found anyone else to play.

Mrs Tennant was half-lying, half-sitting on the sofa, her back supported by cushions, her left leg stretched full-length and encased in a tightly-wrapped bandage from mid-calf to just above the knee. She was still wearing her favourite powder-blue sports dress – the one, she'd laughingly admitted to a friend in Damian's hearing, designed to show off legs as long and slim as hers.

'What've you done?' he inquired sympathetically, not immediately alarmed.

'Stupid, really,' she answered, wrinkling her nose with irritation and lowering the fashion magazine she'd been glancing at to take her mind off the pain. 'Pulled some muscle or twisted some funny ligament or *something* of that sort – nothing that won't mend, eventually.'

Damian sank down on his sports bag opposite the sofa and tried to assess her mood. She could be quite offhand about things that were really important to her and to her family.

'So how did it happen?'

'To be honest, I still don't really know. I went up for a smash and Marion says I just sort of keeled over as I landed. Never seen anything like it,' she added with a humourless laugh. 'Trust me! Really, I put it down to those new sports shoes. I should have known better because they simply didn't feel right before I even started the match. I ought to have kicked them out – literally! But, well, they're a lovely design, really neat and sporty . . .'

'Is it, er, very painful?'

'Certainly was when it happened! And afterwards. Easing off a bit now, thank goodness. And thank goodness, too, Jenny was there this morning and had her doctor's bag with her! She was really gentle and thoughtful. I can see now why her patients rave about her. Anyway, she put on this support bandage and she's sure nothing's broken. But she thinks I should have it checked out at the hospital in the morning. Worse thing is, I definitely won't be able to drive for a bit – maybe as long as a fortnight. Luckily Marion's driven my car heaps of times so she didn't mind bringing me back and Lynsey drove here too so that she could take Marion home. So . . .'

The implications of this disaster had filtered through Damian's sympathy but somehow he managed to hold back the vital question until his mother's narrative rambled to a kind of conclusion.

'But, Mum, what about getting me to United's next match? I mean, you know we've got to play every match away from home from now on. Wheels are essential, you said so yourself. And you promised, promised faithfully, you know you did.'

'Faithfully' had always been one of Sue Tennant's

favourite words. If she used it in relation to a promise then that promise had to be kept whatever the consequences. Her only son had always known that.

She looked pained as she regarded him with sorrowful eyes. 'Darling, *of course* I haven't forgotten my promises. I was really looking forward to seeing you playing in all those funny places I've never been to. But, well, if I can't drive, I can't drive, can I? And so we'll have to make other arrangements. Don't worry, we will, I promise.'

He tried to swallow his frustration and ignore the fact that she hadn't added 'faithfully' this time. In the past, she had usually dropped him and one or two of his team-mates at the match venue and then gone on to play badminton or tennis or whatever else had captured her sporting enthusiasms. And, usually, he'd been given a lift home by another parent. His father, inconveniently, was working in South America for at least six months; and Damian couldn't think of anyone else who'd be able to help out if his mother failed him.

'But who can we ask?' he inquired desperately. '*Who*, Mum?'

She moved slightly on the sofa as if trying to find a more comfortable spot and momentarily her face contorted with pain. Grimacing, she stretched out her other leg. Damian wondered if he should offer to help make her more comfortable. How long would she lie there: an hour, the rest of the day, all *night*? He might have to become a sort of hospital nurse, at her beck and call day and night. And tomorrow evening United had a training session, though where it was to be held still had to be decided.

'Darling, do you think you could fetch me a glass of fizzy orange? I could do with something stronger but Jenny said I should keep off boozy stuff. She gave me some pretty powerful painkillers as part of the treatment.'

Rather unfairly, he knew, he wondered whether she'd asked for the drink just to avoid answering his question. Without a word, he got up and went into the kitchen.

Seeing the basket of fruit beside the store cupboard, he suddenly felt pangs of hunger. After a match he usually was hungry, and now he was ravenous. After pouring the drink for his mother and handing it over with the unanswerable message, 'Be back in a second,' he squashed up a couple of bananas and spread them over slices of buttered wholemeal bread; and, as an afterthought, he filled a bowl with cornflakes adding milk, sugar, slices of pineapple and a few desolate strawberries from the fridge for good measure. With his mother's mobility so severely reduced, it might be some time before she prepared a proper meal for him.

'That looks like sensible eating,' she said approvingly as he sat down once more on the squashed sports bag (now a bit uncomfortable but the most convenient seat from which to talk to her). 'I'll do my best to hobble back into action as soon as I feel up to it but you might have to help out a bit in the kitchen. In fact, when you've finished that little snack I wouldn't mind a cheese sandwich myself. I skipped breakfast today. I need some protein, I think.'

'Were you, er, winning when you hurt your leg?' Damian inquired politely.

'Brilliantly! Truthfully, I really was. I felt good this morning, as well, and I just knew I'd hit top form.' She paused and sighed theatrically. 'But isn't that life? I mean, if only we *really* knew what we were in for . . .'

Damian nodded, his mouth too full of banana to speak. Funny, in a way, but he, too, was sure when he'd got up that he'd be in good form. Must be something to do with the fact that he and his mother were related, he supposed! Still, it had never occurred to him that he would score a goal. That was a definite bonus.

'Darling, I'm sorry, I never asked!' Her hand was at her mouth, her blue eyes wide with mock embarrassment. 'How did YOU get on – your team, I mean?'

He swallowed the food in his mouth. 'We got a point and I scored the second goal, the last one *ever* at the Fold. And we came back from two down, so we did pretty well, really. Not as good as winning, but . . .'

'Good, good.' She seemed genuinely pleased; often, Damian felt, she didn't take in anything he told her about United, or if she did, it was swiftly forgotten. 'Actually, they were talking about the Fold at the Club today. Kelly Whats-her-name was saying that the houses they're building are going to be really luxurious affairs, four bedrooms, two bathrooms, security lighting, landscaped gardens, goodness knows what else. And they're ploughing up the first sods, or whatever it's called, on Tuesday. Funny day to start. Did you know that?'

'Naturally,' he answered emphatically. 'There can't be anything I don't know about our football field. I mean, I *have* been following up every bit of news I could find since we first heard it was to be developed.'

'Sorry, darling,' she said, sounding contrite.

'Listen, I had a thought this morning, a bad one: well, I mean, if it happens, it'll be bad, terrible, really. You know the firm that's just agreed to sponsor us, Empsons?'

'The seed merchants – yes, what about them? Surely they haven't gone back on their word to pay for new kit, not after all the trouble you and Alex took to get them to help?'

'I'm just afraid they might do,' Damian admitted in a low voice. 'I mean, their big factory or whatever they call it is in Redbourne, isn't it, and we're hardly ever going to be playing here. They won't want to advertise themselves in places like, well, Turkdean. I mean, that's in the middle of nowhere! I really like their slogan on our shirts. Go for Growth.'

'Oh no, I don't think you need worry about that,' she said, sounding very positive. 'Empsons trade all over the county – and further afield. In a way, they're probably glad you're playing away because then you'll be spreading the word about them to all corners.'

'A growing market, you mean?' he remarked, grinning at his own pun.

'Oh, very good, Damian! I like it. Honestly, I'm glad there's something to smile about today. Listen, about transporting you to to these away matches: I'll ask Marion if she's got any ideas. Or, come to think of it, maybe Lynsey could – '

She stopped because the telephone started to ring. They both turned to face the hall. Mrs Tennant had resolutely refused to consider installing a mobile phone in the house.

'Look, I expect it's for me but, honestly, I don't feel like talking to anyone at this minute, not even Marion,' she resumed. 'So, darling, do you mind? Just say I'm resting but I'm not at death's door – yet.'

Reluctantly, he put down the bowl of cornflakes and went to pick up the receiver. To his great surprise, the call was for him.

'Damian, hello, this is Bob Snowball. How're you?'

'Fine, Mr Snowball, thanks.' Why was Warren's dad ringing him? Immediately his instinct told him that something was wrong.

'Good, good. Hear you scored a cracking goal this morning.'

'Er, well, it was only a penalty, you know. I

mean, nobody should miss a *penalty* kick.'

'Ah, but they do, don't they? Glad you didn't because Warren said United deserved a point at least. Just sorry I wasn't there to see the game.'

There was a definite pause and Damian didn't know what to say, or even whether he was expected to say anything. Mr Snowball was one of the team's best supporters and often brought Warren to matches in his car and would then give several of them a lift home. However, because of his unusual job he wasn't always free when he hoped to be: he worked for the Customs and Excise and was often away searching ships for hidden drugs or other contraband.

'Look, Damian, I'm afraid I've got some bad news for you,' he resumed. 'Warren's had an accident and he may not be able to play for the team for a while. Certainly he won't be fit for your training session on Tuesday.'

Damian was bewildered. 'But – but – he was fine when we all went off home after the match. I mean, he didn't get a knock or anything. No injury at all. So –'

'Hang on, hang on! My fault, I wasn't explaining things very well. I'm still a bit shaken by what happened.' To Damian that was a chilling phrase. 'It was Jessica's fault, really, though we can't blame her. You know, Warren's little sister. Well, she was trying out this bike we got her for her birthday. Of course, she didn't look exactly where she was going or think about who might be coming round the

corner of our drive. So she went full tilt into Warren, just as he was coming in. He must've put out his hand to save himself when he went over – and, bingo, he's broken his wrist, hasn't he? And jarred his shoulder and generally got himself pretty shaken up, poor lad.'

'Oh no! That's terrible! Is he, well, in lots of pain? Will he have to stay in hospital?

'No, no, we don't think so – not about staying in hospital, that is. Actually, I'm ringing from there now – in the car park, using the car phone. Warren was anxious to let you know what'd happened so you wouldn't count on him turning out in the next match.' There was a very brief pause but Damian hadn't time to marshal his thoughts before Mr Snowball resumed. 'He was really insistent on that and I was impressed that he could think of the football team at a time when he was in a fair bit of pain. But United means a lot to him, Damian, as I expect you know.'

'Er, yes, I do know, Mr Snowball.' That wasn't strictly true. Warren had joined them only at the end of the previous season and there were times when Damian suspected that the tall midfielder with a depth of talent wasn't as interested in soccer as his captain wanted him to be. Perhaps he'd been wrong about that. 'We're going to miss him. I mean, he's a very good player.'

'I'm glad to hear you say that. Often he doesn't seem to believe in himself. But it's my opinion you've been helping to build up his confidence,

Damian. You've shown *you* believe in him – and that's important. Anyway, I'd better get back to the casualty department and see how things're getting along. I'm hoping we can all get off home pretty soon. Glad to catch you in, Damian. Cheers, then.'

'Oh, Mr Snowball, just a second!' Damian put in hastily. 'Will it be all right if I drop round to see Warren, bring him some books or something, you know, to cheer him up?'

'That's kind of you, Damian, very thoughtful. I know he'll be thrilled to see you any time. But not today, though. Give him time to, well, adjust. OK then, look forward to seeing you.'

Damian put down the receiver and wandered back into the sitting room, reflecting on the latest grisly news for Darton United. His mother had picked up a fashion magazine but he didn't think she was really reading it.

'Well,' he announced in a tone of deep gloom, slumping on to his sports bag yet again, 'I think there's a jinx on Darton United, I really do. I mean, it's just one bad thing after another – no end to them. Honestly, I feel like giving up, packing the game in like that Liverpool manager when he'd had enough.'

She managed a wan smile when he'd finished. 'There is one thing that might bring you a bit of comfort.'

He frowned. 'What's that?'

'Usually, bad luck goes in threes – I'm sure you've heard that before. Well, I reckon you've now had

34

your trio: losing your pitch to a housing development, my leg injury which'll make it difficult to get you and some of your buddies to these away matches, and Warren's broken wrist. After all that, surely life will get a bit easier for your team?'

Damian made no reply. His instinct told him that although there might be some truth in that there was also something illogical in what his mother had just said.

THREE

Death of a Canary

With increased vigour, Damian scrubbed away at the large patch of dried mud on the off-side front wing of the car. He'd noticed the owner of the Ford studying him from an upstairs window and he didn't want the man to think he wasn't trying hard enough to remove every scrap of dirt from the car. 'Spotless, and nothing less, that's what I want it to be,' he'd demanded – and Damian was determined to provide the perfect car cleaning service. He suspected that if the man could detect any imperfections in the work then he was just the sort to withhold part of the payment.

It wasn't coming off. So it wasn't mud after all. It could be tar if he'd recently travelled along a newly-surfaced road; or maybe he'd driven into a farmyard and the stain was from something even worse. Damian wrinkled his nose. This was one of the worst bits of the job, not knowing what you'd find stuck to a vehicle. He rubbed again, but not too fiercely because the worst disaster of all would be to damage the paintwork. Some owners could become almost hysterical if they feared you might scratch anything. They were always men; women, in Damian's experience, really didn't mind what you did so long as the car looked reasonably clean.

He stood up and stepped back to examine his handiwork: the scarlet Sierra really was gleaming now, apart from a minute spot of dried soap which he promptly removed from a wing mirror. Really, there could be no excuse whatsoever for denying him so much as one penny of the £1.50.

'Well done, well done, that looks good, *really* good,' exclaimed the owner, bustling out of the house and taking Damian by surprise in several respects. 'It's a long time since it looked as good as that.'

'Oh, er, thank you, thanks very much,' responded Damian. He knew he shouldn't point out any shortcomings but his conscience would trouble him if he didn't. 'But I couldn't manage to clean off that mark on the wing just here.'

The man laughed. 'I should think not, not with just soapy water, anyway! That's paint from the car of the stupid idiot that bumped into me this week. No damage done to me but he's getting the bill for leaving his mark on me, I can tell you. Sorry I didn't mention it before you started. Anyway, here's your money.'

'But this is fifteen pence more than I asked for,' said Damian, holding out the extra coins on the palm of his hand.

Shaking his head to show he didn't want them

back, the Sierra driver continued to smile. 'You keep it, son. If one of my sales force does a particularly good job he can earn a ten per cent bonus. I reckon you deserve the same today. Can you come back next week, same time? I'll get my wife's car out for you then, as well. Hers doesn't get as mucky as mine.'

'Definitely!' Damian emptied his bucket of water over the nearest flowerbed and then hooked it over the handlebars of his bike before stowing away his sponges, polishing cloths and liquid soap container in a saddlebag. It was satisfying to think he'd have two customers at this house the following week.

'Hope your team wins on Sunday – and that you raise plenty of money,' was the man's parting shot. Damian waved his thanks as he accelerated away, heading now for the Canary Café. After a hard day at school and then cleaning half a dozen cars, he felt he deserved a rest and a chance to discuss plans with his United team-mates.

The café in Redbourne town centre had long been a favourite haunt of Damian's, and several important meetings in the short history of Darton United had taken place there while the players tucked into choice cakes and drinks. Recently, though, it had changed ownership and the new proprietor wasn't so welcoming.

Damian parked his bike as usual in the yard at the rear of the building and had to move carefully to avoid heaps of rubble and piles of what looked like chopped-up wood; it took him a moment or two

to identify the remains of the old-fashioned wooden tables and ancient church pews that had helped to give a historic touch to the café. He raised his eyebrows, wondering what he was going to find instead.

'Hi, Damian, good to see you – thought you weren't going to make it tonight,' he was greeted by Alex Anson, seated at a parrot-green table, a colour that shrieked at the senses almost as loudly as the bird itself. Damian paused to take in the scene, registering that the individual seats, plainly attached to the floor, were in a shade that matched oranges in California. The overall hue was a shock to the system, though nobody else was actually shielding his eyes against the glare.

'Looks great now, doesn't it?' remarked Paul Merchant, United's moon-faced full-back who clearly had rediscovered his old appetite judging by the amount of food on his plate. 'And these toasted sandwiches are terrific – lashings of that sweet'n'sour stuff in the middle, as well.'

Danny Clixby was the only other member of the team present but he didn't say a word because his mouth was full of sausage and baked beans, not the sort of dish that had ever been served in the old Canary Café. But he raised a thumb to show approval of something or other as Damian made his way to the counter to order a wedge of irresistible coffee cake and a Coke.

The drink was readily available – the glass-fronted icebox seemed to be stacked full of red and white cans – but coffee cake was no longer on the menu. 'Got a different supplier now,' the girl assistant told him, pointing to a selection of slices, each individually wrapped in transparent film. She was new, too, slim and dark and pretty with bright red lips and huge, dangly earrings. 'There's fruit cake and cherry cake and banana cake and, well, all sorts, whatever you like.'

Sighing, he settled for the banana confection, which proved to be almost twice the price of the coffee cake; naturally it wasn't as good but Damian would have admitted, if pressed, it wasn't bad either. Still, nobody could spoil a *banana*. After working so hard for his money he was reluctant to spend it on anything but the best, and if he was to be true to his word, it wasn't really his money to spend.

'Hey, you're loaded!' Danny exclaimed, his dark brown eyes opening wide as he caught sight of the money Damian was rearranging in his wallet. 'Why didn't you get yourself more than just one measly bit of cake? You could afford to get a bit for all of us – make mine that one full of cherries!'

The other boys laughed but Damian didn't. 'That's not really my money, even though I've just earned it, washing cars. That's why I'm late.' He shot a glance at Alex, remembering his vice-captain's greeting. 'This money is all for the Save United Fund.'

'I thought we were quite healthy, didn't know we were in danger of, well, *dying*,' Paul put in, but nobody thought that was funny. The long-serving full-back had such a peculiar sense of humour some people suspected he had no idea what the word humour meant, anyway.

'Merch, you *have* heard we've lost our ground and are now homeless, haven't you?' Alex inquired with obvious sarcasm. 'I mean, some of us think that's a bit of a problem and we just might go out of business if we don't find somewhere else pretty smartly.'

'Oh, yeah, of course. Sorry. Sorry, Damian.' He really did sound contrite, so Damian didn't say anything. In any case, he knew he could always rely on Paul's support when it was really needed. He suddenly realised, though, that he ought to have mentioned his idea of starting a fund to Alex. In the previous United crisis, when Ian Venn had tried to wrest the captaincy away from him and sow discord throughout the team, Alex had displayed strength of purpose and ingenuity as well as personal loyalty to Damian himself.

'I just had this brainwave today that we should start up a sort of fighting fund,' Damian hurriedly explained, stretching the truth only a little. 'You know, if we can show people we're doing something for ourselves, well, maybe they'll be ready to help us. My mum agrees: she says people will dig into their pockets and purses if they see that someone else has started the ball rolling – if you see what I mean. But they don't want to be the first. That's in case they're the only ones, I suppose. So . . .'

'Good thinking,' Alex said approvingly, to Damian's relief. 'Wish I'd thought of it. It could really give us a big boost all the way round.'

'But, er, what do we want the money *for*?' asked Paul rather tentatively, as if afraid that it was a stupid question.

'Well, lots of things, actually,' United's captain replied positively. 'For a start, it costs parents and other people more money now to take us to all these away matches. To show we're glad of what they're doing for us it would be nice if we could offer to pay for the petrol now and again. It'd show our *appreciation*.'

'Doesn't mean to say they'd take it just 'cos we'd offered it,' pointed out Danny, his plate now empty, allowing him to devote all his attention to the conversation. 'Like *my* mum says, it's the thought that counts!'

They laughed at that while recognising the truth of it. Alex, who'd been looking further ahead, had another suggestion.

'We could use some of the money to put an advertisement in the evening paper. You know, sort of : "Wanted: good football pitch on Sundays for top junior side. Urgent. Phone Damian Tennant." Then we'd put your number in. Might get a lot of interest that way.'

Damian nodded. 'Not a bad idea at all, Alex. Except I have an idea ads in a newspaper these days cost a fortune. A neighbour of ours told Mum that he wanted to advertise his old car the other day but when he learned how much it'd cost he said it wasn't worth it. He wouldn't get that much for the car!'

'But maybe we could give the newspaper a *story* about ourselves. We'd get that *free* and save the cost of an advert,' said Danny, becoming more inventive by the minute. 'They could do a real sob story on us, about how we've had our pitch torn up by thundering great bulldozers.'

'Well, the paper's already done a story on the housing development and we got a mention,' Paul put in to everyone's surprise. 'It was on page two. My dad showed it to me. I thought everyone'd've seen it. They said something about one of the losers being a junior football side – that meant us. Don't suppose they'll want to do the same story again, will they?'

He looked meaningfully round the table but no

43

one disagreed with him. Clearly, that was an idea that had to be written off!

'Well, there ought to be some other story we can think of that the paper'll want to use,' Alex resumed. 'Football's always in the news – and look at the amount of space they give to Redbourne City, and not just on the sports pages either. I think that if – '

'Hey, we could contact Bryn Marsden at Charlton and ask him to bring his own team to play City in a sort of benefit match for us,' Paul cut in eagerly, his eyes alight at the memory of one of the best days of his life, the day when he was one of the ball boys for City's home match with Plymouth Argyle. Bryn, a City player, had done a lot for Darton United as their coach and president; then, after his transfer to Charlton, he arranged for Damian to be City's mascot* and the rest of the United team to be the ball boys on that unforgettable occasion.

Damian shook his head. 'It's a nice thought, Paul, but I really don't think we'd stand a chance. None of us has been in touch with Bryn for ages and he's probably forgotten us, anyway. City probably have our name on their file or whatever it's called but, again, we haven't kept up our contact with them. Testimonial matches – that's what they're called – are only for big-name players who've been playing for the same club for ten years, or even longer.'

He paused and then seeing the disappointment on

* See *Mascot*

Paul's face, he added: 'Sorry, but it's not on. The only possibility is a charity match for us but I don't think our problem is big enough to get that sort of rating from a top League club.'

The references to top players had sparked an idea in Alex's mind. 'We could write to loads of the big names and ask them if they'd give us something, a tie or a sock or just an autograph perhaps; then we could *auction* everything and raise money that way.'

'I like it, I like it!' Damian responded, grinning at his vice-captain. 'Even if everybody we write to doesn't reply I think plenty will for a good cause like ours. We can organize that pretty quickly, ask every player in our squad to write, what, half a dozen letters each? Won't cost anything really – '

'Not if we ask our parents to pay for the postage,' Danny chimed in. Clearly, Alex reflected, United's new, darting striker had an eye for a money-saving opportunity.

'I'll make a note of these ideas,' Damian said, fishing out a pocket notebook from an inner pocket. 'Can't afford to forget anything that'll help. Right, lads, any more suggestions?'

There was a brief interval while they pondered any possibilities; and it was Paul who eventually came up with one. 'Tin cans,' he declared. 'That's a winner. I know 'cos me and some of my mates did a big collecton once for the scouts. Just any old cans'll do because they're wanted for recycling – it's also a good green project, you know. Also, did you know steel is the only common metal that's attracted to magnets? Means you can get a magnet and work your way through any collection of rubbish in the bins and the old cans'll stick to it. Drink cans, food cans, *baked beans'* cans,' he added, glancing at Danny's empty plate.

'Ugh! Don't fancy that one bit,' Danny replied. 'Rotten job, messing about in other folks' dustbins. Enough to put you off your food!'

'Well, if we can get money for cans that can be recycled then – '

'Oh yes. One *billion* cans are recycled every year – I remember that from the publicity stuff when we were doing our collection,' Paul interrupted eagerly.

' – then, as I say,' Damian went on, 'we should do it. Paul can be in charge of that job, OK? Get it organized properly, Paul, and we can all have a go together one day – or night.'

Paul's face slipped a little as he realised what he might have let himself in for but he nodded; he'd long ago learned that, when Damian was in charge, it was important to think first of what was good for the team.

'Talking of food,' began Alex, which caused Paul's eyes to flicker into life again momentarily, 'my mother wouldn't mind making some for us to sell, I'm sure. You know, if we did have an auction, well, we could also sell refreshments. Mum's terrific at some things, especially vegetarian dishes. So . . .'

'Definitely!' Damian recalled the nut roast and the lemon meringue pie he'd lunched on one day at Alex's home: they were utterly delicious. 'I'll probably want to buy most of 'em myself.'

'Talking of food, as *you* were saying, I've been wondering how long you were thinking of staying, now you've finished eating mine,' a voice remarked behind Damian's right ear. He turned to find a youngish man leaning nonchalantly against the wall, a young man with a rather superior manner and wearing a military-style white tunic over a purple shirt. Damian correctly assumed that he must be the new owner, or at least related to him.

'Er, well, we were just thinking of going, actually,' Damian replied; and then almost immediately he wondered why he was being so weak. As a paying customer, surely he was entitled to sit in the café as long as he liked?

'I don't *want* to turn you out but, as you can see, we are a bit pushed for space,' Purple Shirt stated with the sort of smile that turned into a sneer.

'We never stay where we're not welcome, that's always been our policy – my mum says,' Danny announced loudly as the four of them shuffled out.

It wasn't a bad parting shot and Damian wished he'd thought of something equally cutting: after all, they were practically being turned out. Then Purple Shirt popped up again as Damian scrambled over the junk in the café yard to retrieve his bike.

'I don't want you leaving that bike here again, young fella – this is not a car park, you know,' he was told in a patronising tone. 'Other people will follow you in if they see what you're up to.'

'No chance of that,' Damian replied promptly.

'Don't think I'll be coming here again or my mates, either.'

That pleased him because he'd had the final word; but, at the same time, it was a bit sad to think they wouldn't be returning to the Canary Café. On the other hand, it was no longer the place it had been as Danny confirmed as they all assembled on the pavement on the opposite side of the road before going their separate ways.

'Look, that guy's going to take the sign down, I'll bet anything – he's just taken a ladder off the roof of his van,' he exclaimed excitedly. 'Wonder what it's going to be called now.'

'The Vulture's Rest or something,' Paul predicted, which raised a laugh.

'If the Canary's *dead* it ought to be about a cat that killed it,' said Alex, which was more inspirational. 'How about . . . The Cat-astrophe!'

'Nobody'd eat there if it was called that, you nut,' Damian told him, grinning. It wasn't the worst joke in the world.

'Hang on!' said Danny. 'The guy up the ladder's bound to know, isn't he? I'll nip over and ask him. Don't move, I'll be right back.'

They watched with some amusement, particularly in Alex's case, as Danny dashed across the road and then engaged the sign writer in conversation.

'You're not going to believe this!' declared Danny, panting, as he returned to them, wide-eyed. 'Never in this world. So, go on, have a guess.'

'No point in that, you've just said so yourself,'

Alex pointed out. 'If you won't tell us we might just as well push off home immediately. I've got plenty to do, including some maths homework. I'm not having that on my mind all weekend.'

The other two nodded and so Danny was forced to disclose his news. 'This is it, then: The Tea House of the Rainbow Sky. So how about *that*?'

They were nonplussed and nobody could think of any comment at all until, shaking his head in bewilderment, Paul asked: 'But what does it mean? Doesn't make any sense at all to me.'

'That's just what I wanted to know,' said Danny, thankful that someone had asked. 'The guy *thinks* it means the café will turn out to be a pot of gold at the end of the rainbow – get it? And the Tea House is a sort of trendy name for any place where you can get a cuppa and a cake.'

'But how will he get all that on the signboard?' Paul wondered. 'I mean, it's what, *seven* words. By the time somebody's read all that they won't feel like bothering to go in!'

'Well, that's their problem,' said Danny briskly, pleased to have stirred up so much interest. 'But I've got to go, too. See you Sunday, then.'

Damian was about to ride away, too, when Alex forestalled him. 'Listen, what're we going to do about replacing Warren? I mean, we can't leave it until Sunday, can we?'

'Yeah, I've been thinking about that,' Damian admitted.

'Then I wish you'd share your thoughts with me,'

Alex said sharply. 'I thought we were supposed to plan team tactics and that sort of thing together. I am vice-captain, remember. So . . .'

'Sorry, Alex. I did mean to phone you up and – well, I suppose I've had a lot on my mind, that's all, especially since I had the idea of raising money. Er, have you thought of something, then?'

'I have. I've thought of Ian Venn. Now, hang on! I know what you're going to say: that he walked out on us at the end of last season when we didn't get promotion and he had no chance of taking over as captain again. But he's a good player, you know that, and I know for a fact he isn't playing for anyone else this season. Saw him the other day and he told me he really missed playing for United. Damian, I'm sure as anything that Ian wouldn't try again to get the captaincy off you. He *knows* we're all solidly behind you. He said that, too.'

For a moment Damian didn't make any reply. Ian had been captain of United once, but only briefly; almost as soon as he took over the job he broke his leg in a training accident and Damian replaced him. Then, when Ian recovered and returned to the team, Damian had never offered him the captaincy back, mainly because he himself was enjoying the role and he knew he had the team's support. From time to time, however, his conscience had troubled him and he believed he should have done more the previous season to make Ian feel he had an important part to play in United's future.

'What do you think, Paul?' Damian inquired,

much to the full-back's surprise. Because it was he who was really responsible for Ian's fracture, though everyone had accepted that it was an accident. Nonetheless, he could recall only too vividly the horrors of that moment and his own feeling of responsibility.

'Er, well, I, er, agree with Alex. Ian is a good player and we definitely need somebody who can play a bit to take over from Warren. I mean, we haven't a pool of spare players we can dive into when we need one, have we?' He was rather pleased with that phrase: and still more pleased to be consulted over team selection. Perhaps Damian and Alex had a higher opinion of him than he'd imagined. Paul awarded them his most genial smile.

'OK, then, let's see if he wants to play for United again,' Damian said decisively. 'I'll get in touch and see what – '

'I'll do it, I'll do it, Damian,' Alex butted in eagerly. 'I told you, I was with him recently so I know he'll agree. Leave it to me and he'll be with us on Sunday, I'm sure of it.'

Damian wasn't going to argue but it did cross his mind that Alex might have some other motive for getting Ian to rejoin United. On the other hand, Alex had proved his loyalty to United many times and Damian couldn't believe he'd do anything to undermine his own leadership. At a time like this, with their future threatened through the loss of their home ground, they had enough to worry about without facing personality problems.

'Any ideas about how we're going to beat Turkdean on Sunday?' he inquired, mounting his bike but keeping abreast of his team-mates as they walked in the direction of their homes, both much nearer to the café than his own.

'One thing we've got to do is keep an eye on a lad of theirs called Gee Tullock – he's pretty rough, I'm told,' said Alex, whose information network about the local leagues was extensive and much admired by his friends. 'Plays up-front usually so we've got to close him down. Maybe we could get Ian to do it. I know he likes going forward but he can shackle opponents when he has to.'

'Sounds a good idea,' put in Paul, who was increasingly feeling part of the United management team. 'Is Gee his real name or what?'

'Well, I heard he was always telling his own team to "Gee up" and so they started called him Gee,' Alex explained. 'Seems he likes the name so it's stuck. Don't know what his real first name is.'

'OK, well, I'll think about it,' responded Damian, determined to make the final decisions himself. 'Listen, I'll give you both a buzz tomorrow night and we'll sort out the team and the travel arrangements. See you.'

'He does get worried, doesn't he?' Alex remarked as they watched Damian's rapid progress down the road. 'Keeps things bottled up too much. He should relax more. Everything's going to turn out fine for United. I'm sure of it.'

'Oh, I agree completely, Alex,' said Paul with the

air of someone who now expected to be involved in cabinet-style discussions – and thoroughly enjoyed the experience.

FOUR

Trouble at Turkdean

The car was even better than Damian had hoped it might be: a gleaming black BMW saloon with its numberplate bearing the latest annual index letter. As it drew up in front of his gate, where he'd been patiently waiting for eleven minutes, he really could fantasise about being chauffeured to his club's top match in a personal limousine supplied by the Chairman of the Board of Directors. After all, the person at the wheel was a stranger to him and she had come to his address just to pick him up.

The image was spoilt by just two facts: Neil Dallimore was already sprawled in the back and Damian knew the name of the driver because she was a friend of his mother's and generously had agreed to ferry a party of United players to their away match with Turkdean.

'Hello, Damian, hope you haven't been waiting long,' Lynsey Poole greeted him with the sort of smile that always obliterated the risk of criticism from males of any age. 'We reserved the front seat for the captain – so hop in. That's my daughter in the back with Neil. Elinor's quite a football fan herself, you'll find.'

'Hi,' she called out with a warmth that almost matched her mother's. She was, Damian noted when he turned to smile at her, quite small with shoulder-length auburn hair and was wearing rectangular, rimless glasses. 'Hope your team's going to score a big win today. That's what I've come to see. Fact is, Mum couldn't keep me away when I knew where she was going. So don't let me down.'

'We'll, er, try not to,' replied Damian. 'We need the points pretty badly if we are to get promotion this season. Turkdean are a tough team, though.'

It crossed his mind that Elinor might fancy playing for United. A lot of girls nowadays were keen on soccer, including some at his own school, but he'd yet to see one good enough for United. But he must be careful not to say anything hurtful to her if that was her ambition: after all, they needed all the help available to transport players to matches.

'How is your mother, Damian?' Mrs Poole inquired, almost as if she'd been reading his mind and wanted to steer any conversation away from the subject of girls playing for boys' teams. 'I intended to drop in and say hello but we were held up at roadworks – yes, even on a Sunday, would you believe? So I didn't want to delay your journey any longer.'

'Oh, much better, thanks, Mrs Poole. She's hobbling about a bit now and talking of starting to drive again – wants to go to some reunion of her old class-mates or something like that in Brighton.'

Lynsey Poole laughed. 'Sounds just like her. Very sociable person, your mum, Damian. I expect she'll be chauffeuring you again in no time.'

'Won't be in a car as good as this, though,' remarked Neil, thinking he'd been silent long enough. 'This is really great. Is it yours, Mrs Poole?'

'Definitely not!' Elinor replied before her mother could speak. 'It's Dad's and he drives it *twice* as fast – no, three times. Mum's really slow.'

Slow or not, she got them to the Turkdean ground well ahead of everyone else from the Darton area, for which Damian was thankful. He wanted to be on hand to greet Ian and make sure that everyone else welcomed him back into the team, even though he'd passed on that message by phone to practically all his team-mates the previous evening.

Ian was one of the players being picked up by Bob Snowball, who'd insisted on helping out even though his son wasn't able to play and didn't even feel able to watch. ('Warren's a terrible spectator,' his father confided to Damian. 'He lives every kick and would probably do himself an injury in the excitement.') However, Mr Snowball intended to stay and watch whereas Mrs Poole, after dropping off her passengers, promptly departed to see an old friend thus proving that she, too, was a very sociable person. Elinor declared that she'd come to see the football and wandered off on her own to stand behind one of the nets, confirming Damian's suspicions that she had motives apart from spectating.

Alex and Hajinder were among the players in Mr Snowball's car and as they went over to confer with Damian they flanked Ian like bodyguards.

'Good to have you back with us,' Damian said as cheerfully as he could manage. He thought Ian looked a bit sullen and he'd grown his hair long again, which somehow made him look older.

'Thanks,' replied Ian, but that was all he said. Alex had already explained where and how they wanted him to play.

Damian's attention was caught by Turkdean who were wearing one of the most colourful outfits he'd seen: orange shirts with diagonal red and blue stripes and black shorts trimmed with red.

'Look like a box of Turkish Delight or something,' Bob Snowball remarked to no one in particular; but hardly anyone who heard him had ever seen the gooey sweets he was referring to. But it didn't take him long to realise there weren't many soft centres among the home players.

Gee Tullock, Turkdean's strutting leader, long-faced and with a prominent nose, stationed himself just behind the strikers at the kick-off in much the same position Ian occupied for United. Although the football ground was some distance from the village the home side had plenty of support and they gave them a rousing cheer when the young referee blew his whistle and waved the teams into action. Immediately, Neil Dallimore hoofed the ball out to the right wing for Stevie Pailthorp to chase and then hit back into the middle.

Anticipating such a cross, Danny moved sharply to chest the ball down, take it on for a couple of strides and then, cleverly, slide it sideways for Ian Venn to run on to and try a shot. And that shot was on target: in spite of being taken almost by surprise, the Turkdean goalie got his hands to the ball, managing to push it out for a team-mate to stab it over the dead-ball line before Danny, following up, could reach it.

Elinor, who was standing beside the near post, clapped her hands vigorously. 'Great start, Homeless United! Keep it up!'

'What!' exclaimed a home supporter, mishearing her. 'Hopeless United? They don't look hopeless to me.'

Laughing, Elinor explained that he'd got it wrong, that United had lost their own ground but were determined to overcome such obstacles.

'Well, in that case, they certainly need supporters like you to cheer 'em on,' the man observed. 'Teams usually perform better when the crowd's behind 'em. How many more have you brought with you?'

Elinor looked round but quickly stopped counting. 'Just two, I think. But I'm sure they've got a lot of fans in Darton.'

Damian had raced to take the corner kick himself, eager that not a moment should be wasted when his team had started so well. With the slight aid of a light wind, the ball floated to the edge of the box where Matthew Morgan, United's tall central defender, moved sharply to head it on into the goalmouth. Neil lunged for it, failed to make contact . . . a Turkdean player missed his kick completely when he swung at the ball . . . the goalie, still on his line, dithered . . . and Ian Venn hurled himself forward to nudge the ball over the line with his left temple.

Within eighty seconds of the start of the match, Darton United were a goal up.

'A dream start,' Damian murmured, stating the obvious; but it didn't matter because no one was listening to anything he said. Ian had practically disappeared under a deluge of congratulations with team-mates leaping on him to express delight and let him know how much they welcomed his return.

'Come on, lads, come on, it's only the first goal, you know, not the winner in a cup final,' complained the referee, himself detaching some of the limpets from around Ian's neck. 'I wish you'd all stop aping those over-paid superstars you see on the telly.'

Damian restricted himself to a slap on the back for Ian but made a point of saying a word or two of praise to Matthew, one of United's newer recruits. After all, it was his enterprising header that had chiefly led to the goal-scoring chance. Matthew beamed. Secretly, he hoped that one day Damian would want to play him at centre-forward; and then, Matthew vowed, he'd score a stack of goals.

'Well, that's really fast work,' remarked Elinor's

new friend, the home supporter. 'Don't remember when I saw a quicker goal than that to start a match. D'you *always* play like this, then?'

'Er, no, not always,' admitted Elinor, hoping she wasn't being unfair or disloyal to United. But she wasn't going to confess to never having seen them in action before today. She'd been thinking about the man's earlier comment about support for the team; it was true, they did deserve a fan club. Mentally, she flicked through a list of her friends, ticking off the names of those she thought would be interested in the players. After all, some of them were really nice-looking boys and she herself was beginning to admire Damian; for one thing, he wasn't too tall, unlike Neil, the first United player she'd met. The gangling striker didn't seem nearly as intelligent as the team's sturdy, dark-haired captain.

At that moment the captain was plotting how to capitalise on his team's brilliant start to another vital game. From past experience, he knew that Ian Venn would now want to go forward all the time; he'd always believed he should really be a striker. But Damian needed him in midfield in place of Warren, going up with the attack only occasionally. With Stevie, Neil and Danny in full flow United had quite enough attackers most of the time, especially as Damian himself enjoyed a foray in the box now and again. However, Turkdean had plainly been rocked by the speed of the opening goal, so it was essential for United to increase the pressure on the opposition.

In predictable fashion, Gee Tullock tried to barge his way through United's defence when fed by one of his own midfielders. Alex was the player sent sprawling and although normally he was the last to protest about foul play, this time he even attempted to retaliate, as he had received a particularly painful blow in the groin. The referee sympathised and while Alex started to wander round, bent double but refusing assistance of any kind, United were awarded a free kick just on the perimeter of the centre circle.

Paul Merchant, whose strength had been developing well lately, pumped the ball hard towards the Turkdean penalty area. Inevitably, Neil Dallimore went for the ball, only to be beaten to it by a defender; but his heading ability was poor and when the ball bounced away at an unexpected angle Ian pounced. Shielding the ball cleverly from crude tackles, he rounded an opponent, flicked the ball to Danny, called for a one-two, got it back – and fired in a blistering shot.

Once again, the goalie managed to parry the shot but couldn't hold the ball: he tried to dive on it but succeeded only in pushing it into the path of the in-rushing Ian. With commendable coolness the United midfielder took the ball under control, swerved past the stricken keeper and, almost offhandedly, slid it into the unguarded net before the nearest full-back could get near him.

Four minutes gone and United now *two* goals up.

Ian couldn't contain his excitement. Wheeling

away, arms aloft, he ran towards the nearest green shirts, the ones worn by Neil and Danny and, joining them fast, Stevie. All the rest of the United players seemed to want to swamp him, too, and moments later all that could be seen of the goal scorer was a little of his straw-coloured hair. Only Damian and Paul, and, of course, Hajinder, weren't in the scrum. Damian was actually looking at the referee, worrying a little about the legitimacy of the goal in case there was any risk of its being offside, when Alex got to his feet.

'He's injured, he's really hurt!' he called.

The referee, perfectly happy about the goal as it happened, was writing in his notebook; but instantly he pocketed notebook and pen and raced across to see what was wrong. The despair in Alex's voice alarmed him.

'No, no!' Damian said fervently between gritted teeth. 'Not another break, not *another* one, please!' But in his heart, he knew it was.

'*Don't* crowd around – that's the worst thing,' the referee was telling everyone. Young he might be, but he had an air of complete authority. He was obeyed at once, players drawing back and, some at least, looking guiltily at one another.

Damian had seen Ian when his leg was broken in Paul's tackle and Ian's face was just as white now as it had been then. Biting his lip to help him control the pain, he was gripping his right arm just above the wrist. Bob Snowball, who'd been patrolling the touchline, now darted on to the pitch to see what he

could do – and one glance was enough to tell him
he'd have to make another trip to the nearest
hospital casualty department.

'Come on, son, we'll get that attended to right
away,' he said calmly to Ian after putting his jacket
round the boy's shoulders. 'It might just be severe
bruising, so don't – '

'No, it won't – it's broken, I know,' Ian, now
trembling slightly with shock, replied abruptly.
'They said before when I broke my leg that my
bones might be, well, sort of, brittle.'

'I'm very grateful, very grateful indeed,' the referee
told Bob Snowball before he got into his car.

'Parents should always be present at matches like these – you never know what's going to happen next. But mostly everything's left to the officials to clear up . . .'

Nobody pointed out that Mr Snowball wasn't the parent of any of the players present: and nobody had apologised to Ian because no one knew exactly who'd been responsible. In a way, they all were because they'd all piled on top of the goal-scorer in the excitement of the moment. Of course, the referee had something to say about it before the match resumed.

'You see what your stupidity led to?' he asked bitterly. 'A broken arm – it looked like a fracture to me. And all because you acted like idiots. I know a goal is exciting but you don't have to go mad. Now I'm warning you for the last time: another scene like that, by *either* side, and there'll be a few yellow and red cards, I promise you. Got it?'

Both teams were too shaken by what they'd seen before Ian was led away that nobody so much as grinned or tried to look unconcerned as often happened when officials delivered lectures about players' conduct during a match. One boy nodded vigorously as if he supported every word he'd heard: Paul Merchant. But, as much as anything, that was in relief that this time he wasn't in any way responsible for the injury to Ian. He remembered how he'd felt when Ian's leg was broken and Paul was thankful he didn't have to go through that again.

Damian's problems included the use of United's substitute, Mark Scott, who'd only played one game for the team so far and hadn't displayed much promise on that occasion or in training sessions. Simply because United were short of players generally Mark, who seemed able to use only one foot, was encouraged to keep turning up. As he was the only substitute available it would mean United were down to ten players if anyone else were hurt during the remainder of the match.

'Scottie, take over at the back,' the skipper instructed him. 'I'm moving Alex into the middle alongside me. Just do your best and don't waste the ball when you get it. OK?'

Surprisingly, Mark didn't mind being called 'Scottie' – he even made jokes about having teeth and a bite as strong as a terrier's. Now, pleased by his sudden promotion, he darted away to join the back four.

'Look, we've got to keep pressing forward,' Damian said to Alex after telling him about the positional switch. 'They'll expect us to sit on our lead but that's no good. If we can score again soon they'll probably fold up completely.'

Alex wasn't convinced about that strategy, especially as he was moving out of defence to be replaced by someone as feeble (in Alex's opinion) as Mark Scott. 'I think we should just play it cool for a bit, not take any risks.'

Damian for once wasn't really listening to his closest ally. He couldn't thrust aside his fear that, for some reason, United were jinxed. Not only had they lost their ground, they were losing players at an alarming rate, first Warren and now Ian (for the second time if his previous misfortune was taken into account). Even his mother's injury had badly affected their usual routine and planning. What, he kept worrying, would go wrong next? At present he had no doubt at all that *something* would.

Some instinct caused him to glance across at Elinor and immediately she saw she had his attention she stuck a thumb up in the air. Damian didn't acknowledge the signal because he couldn't think how to: he knew she wished him and the team well but she'd been aware of the disaster that struck them. Again it flitted through his mind that he might have to call on her; except that it couldn't be in this match because the Redbourne Sunday League administrators insisted that all new players be registered with them before turning out in any match.

Turkdean attacked from the kick-off. In spite of being two goals down, they knew United must be vulnerable after losing a player with a suspected fracture. Their captain sensed that several Darton players could be in a state of shock.

He was right. When Tullock burst out of a melée with the ball Paul Merchant's attempt at a tackle was little more than a token and so the Turkdean striker barrelled on into the penalty area. His shot was well struck too, but the alert Haji was able to knock the ball up and then catch it before his opponent could try again. Nonetheless, Tullock continued his momentum so that he bundled the goalie over. The referee, worried about further serious injuries, rushed up to reprimand the offender and flourish the yellow card.

Gee wasn't worried about that; he'd collected bookings aplenty in the past couple of seasons and been suspended a couple of times. He knew his style of play unsettled opponents and thus presented him with better scoring opportunities. Now he noticed that Hajinder was limping around his area, and so he wouldn't relish another collision.

A couple of minutes later Turkdean's heftiest player booted the ball as hard as he could upfield. For some reason Alex, hanging back a little, tried to head it when he should have waited for the bounce and trapped it; the ball soared over his head and Tullock gave chase. Yet again Paul's imitation of a tackle allowed his opponent to go past him effortlessly before switching the ball to a team-mate just inside the box. Haji, hobbling still, for once hesitated – and that was fatal. The boy in possession simply kept going and then, when the goalie tentatively moved a couple of steps towards him, slammed the ball past him into the back of the net. It was a very cool strike indeed and the colourfully attired home side had every reason to celebrate spectacularly. Instead, remembering the referee's strictures on that subject, they accepted the goal without fuss, merely exchanging thumbs-up signals and even polite handshakes.

Damian groaned audibly. The rest of the United team, however, remained silent. That, the skipper knew, was part of the problem: they weren't reacting to danger signals by calling to help each other. They appeared stunned. Alex, who'd tried to make up for his error by racing back in the hope of making a tackle or interception, should have yelled at Haji to come out, to narrow the striker's angle. He hadn't made a sound. Hajinder was a brave keeper with wonderful reflex reactions but sometimes he betrayed a lack of experience.

So, after dominating the game in those opening minutes, United might struggle to keep a grip on their lead. That's what Damian suspected: and he was absolutely right. Within five minutes, Turkdean notched the equaliser.

Although the skipper urged his team to 'Keep on top, keep *going*!' at the re-start United reacted woefully to another surge from the boys in orange, red and blue shirts. Damian himself was guilty of the first error. Delaying his pass because he was looking for someone in a good position to pass to, he was surprised by an opponent who nippily appeared from behind him and flicked the ball from his toes. Before Damian could recover his composure the Turkdean player sped away and then hit a glorious long pass to a team-mate loitering on the left touchline.

In turn, he ran swiftly, completely out-pacing Matthew Morgan when he cut inside. Damian yelled at Stevie Pailthorp, United's fastest player, to give chase, to do *something* to help his defence. Stevie was slow to move and by then it was too late, anyway. Haji, his pain receding, was now coming off his line. The attacker had already decided what he was going to do: he was going to shoot. He had a good view of the target and he intended to hit it – and score his first goal of the season, a goal he felt was long overdue.

Paul, at last coming to life after a lethargic spell, sprinted across the front of the box to intervene and save his side. The attacker was in the act of shooting when Paul reached him and thrust out a leg to block the ball. He was too late but only by a split second. The ball ricocheted from Paul's shin, soared in a high curve over Haji's head and upflung arms, bounced once in front of goal, struck the underside of the crossbar, came down vertically and then, because of the top spin imparted to it in this sequence, fizzed into the back of the net.

Turkdean had equalised through an own goal.

His hands over his face as if to cover his shame, Paul sank to his haunches; Haji, to his great credit, didn't say a word. Really, there was nothing to say. Damian said something, though: 'I can't *believe* it!' But there was Haji, retrieving the ball, and there were the Turkdean players, celebrating ecstatically. They sensed that, now, all the luck was going their way: and it seemed they were right. Even the referee didn't complain about the celebrations, perhaps because this time they didn't go on too long.

In fact, Turkdean should have gone into the lead

almost immediately. Still in a state of shock, United's defence faltered again to allow Tullock a clear sight of goal after he'd broken through but, in his eagerness, he blazed the ball stratospherically over the bar. Then, only a couple of minutes later, Haji saved his side with a wonderfully agile leap to tip the ball over the bar from a long-range surprise shot from the left-winger. At the half-time interval Damian could feel only relief that United were still on level terms with the ascendant opposition. Turkdean's supporters, Elinor could have told him, were confident of what the second half would bring.

Damian didn't even glance in her direction as the team left the pitch, which disappointed her because she wanted to sympathise with him. United, in her view, were the unlucky ones and she wanted the players to know that they had her total support. Already she was planning how she might be able to help them.

'I don't know what to say,' admitted Damian as the team gathered round him while swigging or sipping orange juice or bottled water. It was true. There'd never been an occasion when he couldn't think of appropriate words for the half-time pep talk. 'I know we've had bad luck but we've also played a lot of rubbish. Some of you just aren't *looking* when you pass the ball, you're just getting rid of it, and that's no good at all. If we don't improve in the second half we'll lose this game, that's definite. And we'll've wasted all Ian's good work.'

It was a mistake. Although he didn't realise it immediately, his mention of Ian deepened his team's gloom. They'd tried to forget the injury and the sight of Ian's stricken face as he was led from the pitch; and now the captain had reminded them of that earlier disaster. Even Paul, who wanted to gabble on about how he hadn't meant to put the ball in his own net, was silent. Alex, usually to be relied on for support in all circumstances, was deep in his own thoughts and sharing them with no one.

'Let's get back into this game right *now*,' was all Damian could suggest as United trooped, and Turkdean raced, back on to the pitch for the second half. Inevitably, the home side launched an immediate attack. Even though they failed to score for six minutes their pressure was relentless. Yet when they did score there was still an element of luck about the goal.

A corner kick, cleverly played short, was then hit low into the box where nobody managed to control it. Then the ball cannoned off Alex's right calf as he tried to turn, flew into the path of a striker and all he had to do was to poke it over the line from point-blank range. Turkdean's supporters were enraptured: from being 0–2 their team was now in front 3–2.

That was the way it stayed. It could have been worse because Turkdean missed a penalty, awarded when Haji brought down a striker to prevent a certain goal; but Gee Tullock's kick was lamentable and Haji redeemed himself by gathering the ball easily. It could have been better because United only narrowly missed three scoring chances, two of them falling to Dalli-a-lot who lived up to his name on one occasion. But the ball wouldn't go into the net for the away team.

Damian was too depressed to say a word to anyone. Elinor wanted to say, 'Bad luck!' but the happy home supporter was chattering away to her when the match ended.

'Your team doesn't just look as if it's lost the match,' he remarked. 'They all look as if they've lost a million pounds and found only a penny! Really down and out, just like you said, homeless – and without hope.'

'I have to agree,' said Elinor, who looked every bit as sorrowful as the United players.

FIVE

Unexpected Visitors

As he lay full length on the sofa Damian appeared to be watching the flickering pictures on the TV screen: but his eyes were seeing nothing. The brilliance of the colours of the exotic fish deep in some distant ocean would normally have attracted him: he would have admired the way they moved, their effortless changes of direction and the cameraman's skills in shooting his subjects from such astonishing angles. Instead, his mind returned to the views he'd had earlier in the evening of the Fold, so recently United's home ground. His hopes of playing there again had now vanished for ever.

Great channels had been gouged out of the turf and mounds of earth were everywhere like dunes in a desert. Black and yellow excavators were parked in what had been a penalty area and other trenches, marked out by stakes and lines bearing tiny fluttering pennants, crossed the old centre circle. Goal posts and crossbars were stacked in a heap awaiting some casual timber collector or a funeral pyre. It was the saddest sight he'd ever seen. All the same, he hadn't been able to resist taking a souvenir himself. With a sharp pocket knife he'd sliced away a chunk of a goal post: he'd calculated that when he'd scored his best goal for United the ball had flicked against the post at about that level before entering the net. No one would ever know why he cherished that wooden splinter but *he* would.

Just as the manoeuvrings of the fish didn't register with him, neither did the sound of the doorbell until his mother limped into the room and said mildly that she didn't mind him wasting his time but at least he might answer the door when the callers were for him.

'For me?' he asked bewilderedly. He couldn't imagine who would be calling on him at this time. Most of his friends lived too far away to drop in casually.

All the same, he jackknifed off the sofa to see who'd arrived: and at that moment Neil Dallimore and Stevie Pailthorp stepped hesitantly into the sitting room, both of them looking distinctly ill at ease.

'Hi, fellas, good to see you,' Damian greeted them, trying to be instantly cheerful. Then a sense of reality took over after he'd noted their glum expressions. 'Something wrong?'

'Er, well, we wanted to tell you what we've, er, decided,' replied Stevie, who seemed to have difficulty in looking directly at United's skipper.

'That's right,' muttered Neil, as if feeling the need to present a united front. 'We thought of phoning you up but we decided it was best, fairer, if we just, well, came round to tell you in person. OK?'

Damian made no reply. Whatever was coming, he wouldn't like it, that was obvious. But before the visitors could say anything more Mrs Tennant returned, holding a tray of drinks and sweet biscuits which she placed carefully on a coffee table beside the sofa.

'Dig in, boys,' she invited them. 'If you're anything like Damian, you're always ready to scoff the odd biscuit or five!'

Damian, of course, knew that wasn't true but he didn't correct his mother. He was aware that her arrival on the scene had disturbed his team-mates just as they were coming to the point of the visit. That could work to his advantage if they still had doubts about whatever it was they were planning to do. Deliberately he refrained from helping himself to anything on the tray.

'Look, we'll have to give you this straight,' Neil announced abruptly, suddenly recovering his nerve. 'Stevie and me, we're thinking of quitting United, going off to join another Sunday League team. Sorry, but – well, we don't want to keep playing for a *losing* team.'

'One that's about as lucky as No. 13 or busting a mirror or seeing the new moon through a window,' said Stevie. 'My Auntie Sarah says they're all disasters.'

'Like United are turning out to be,' murmured

Neil, not quite under his breath.

Damian sank down on to the sofa while his guests continued to stand by the TV set. He hadn't known what to expect but this wasn't quite as bad as he'd feared: his imagination had initially raised the spectre of another disabling injury for someone. In the past he'd managed to cope with mutterings of discontent among his players and he supposed this present visit could be put in that category.

'Listen, we're just going through a bad patch, that's all,' he tried to assure them. 'It won't last, I mean, losing our own ground was the disaster – nothing else has been as bad and – '

'Come off it!' Neil brayed. 'What about Warren's broken wrist and Ian's broken arm and getting beat after two goals up? Oh yeah, and then there was Paul's own goal. So what next?'

'I *agree* that things have gone against us,' Damian replied mildly. 'But, as I said, nothing lasts for ever, so we'll start having a bit of luck soon. If we keep playing as we did in the first few minutes against Turkdean we'll zoom up the League, be in a promotion place in no time.'

Stevie was shaking his head vigorously. 'No way, if we go on the defensive like we did after being two goals up. That was crazy!'

Damian was flabbergasted. 'But that's just what we didn't do,' he exclaimed heatedly. 'I mean, I think we should have tightened up, closed their forwards down. But we kept attacking because I thought if we got another goal it'd clinch it for us.

That's why I moved Alex into midfield, to keep the attack going. I was wrong because that just weakened us at the back and – '

'But you told me, *ordered* me, to drop back to mark one of their forwards,' Stevie pointed out. 'So that weakened our *attack*, Damian. I'm an attacker, not a defender – I'll never be one of those. It's not so long ago since you were telling me I should use my speed more, go at defences, you said.'

'No, no, no,' Damian told him, 'it wasn't like that at all. That was just a temporary move, a change of tactics just for a moment or two. Paul was dithering a bit and you've got the speed to get anywhere, so you were the one to stop that guy if anyone could. Stevie, you're a great winger and that's where I'll always want you to play, out wide or up front.'

'Look, never mind about tactics and that stuff,' Neil said forcefully. 'The thing is, we've had enough, Stevie and me. We want to play for a team that wins things, that's going places. United aren't going anywhere – except *away* to every match.' He gave a bark of a laugh at his own witticism but neither of the other boys thought it was funny. 'We can score goals, plenty of 'em, Stevie and me, when we get the right support. But we're not getting it, are we?'

He darted across to snatch another chocolate bourbon while awaiting Damian's reply. Damian didn't know what to say. He had to choose his words carefully or risk losing two good players. At Turkdean he hadn't handled team matters very well and he couldn't afford another mistake now. *United* couldn't afford another mistake.

'I know things haven't been going well for us and I know I've made mistakes,' said Damian slowly, deciding that honesty was the best policy. 'But they *will* get better. Bound to. We've got a great squad and as soon as Warren and Ian are fully fit again we'll shoot up the League table. We've *proved* we can score goals anywhere, so it doesn't matter all that much that we're playing away from home all the time. Who knows, we might even get a new home ground before long. Anything's possible if you just wait a bit, be patient and – '

'Damian, that's a load of rubbish and you know it,' Neil cut in. 'We're all fed up with waiting for things to get better. We should have been promoted last season but we didn't make it. And that bit about a new ground, well, you're just saying it. It's a dream, that's all. But for now, for real, we're in a – a nightmare!'

The lanky striker was so pleased with that unexpected phrase that his beam of delight swept over Stevie, who promptly nodded his agreement. What's more, he could tell that Damian had no answer. United's skipper looked as downcast as if he'd just scored an own goal in a vital cup match.

'But if you leave us you won't be allowed to play for any other team in our Sunday League, you know,' Damian responded at last. A change of tactics seemed to be his only hope of winning this battle for their services; an appeal to their sense of

loyalty to Darton United wouldn't be heeded, he
feared. 'The Redbourne organisers, administrators
or whatever they're called, won't permit transfers in
the middle of the season. You should know that.
Don't you remember, they wouldn't even allow us
to change our name a couple of years ago when we
wanted to be called Sporting Darton or Darton
Dynamos? Alex and Paul and I even went to see the
League secretary at his house but he couldn't do
anything for us. They're dead keen on keeping to
their rules.'

For a moment there was no reply, although Neil
and Stevie exchanged glances and Neil began to
frown, which told Damian that Dalli-a-lot hadn't

thought through his idea of changing sides. Stevie, however, wasn't going to be put off; he'd never liked being told by anyone what he could do and what he couldn't. He believed Damian had become much too bossy lately and the skipper's instruction to him to act as a defender still rankled.

'Somebody'll want us, even if we have to go into another League,' he stated. 'Good players are always in demand, my dad says. I agree with him. If we have to, we'll wait until next season to join another team.'

That was an admission of weakness and Damian spotted it immediately. It must be exploited. 'In that case,' he said calmly, 'you might just as well continue to play for United for the rest of this season. Then you can keep fit, you'll still be playing football – oh yes, and you'll be able to *advertise* yourselves to other teams and their managers if you play well enough. So I reckon you'd better think about that before you do anything, well, stupid.'

The final word caused Neil's frown to deepen and Damian wondered if he'd gone too far; on the other hand, there was little point in letting them think they were being clever and could do whatever they liked. He wondered how a top manager would deal with such a problem. Of course, *he* would have alternatives: if players didn't want to stay then he could instantly put them on the transfer list and get money for them. And then he'd be in a position to sign replacements from other clubs. Life, Damian reflected, must be a lot easier for captains and managers in the Football League itself than it was in the Redbourne Sunday League.

'Okay, we'll think about it,' Neil muttered, much to Damian's surprise. 'But don't you forget, Damian, we're not going to be losers, Stevie and me – no way.'

Damian nodded. 'I won't. But, listen, if you're not going to play in our next match at Mortsea let me know in good time. I'll need to get your replacements fixed up. Ring me by Thursday at the latest.'

His visitors didn't say they would but their silence suggested to him that they'd think carefully before doing anything rash. Neil's weakness for chocolate biscuits overcame his normal standards of behaviour as a guest and he swooped to pick up his fourth bourbon before he and Stevie headed for the front door. In any case, Mrs Tennant *had* invited him to help himself.

Once they'd departed Damian sank back on to the sofa again, lying with his hands behind his head and staring at the ceiling. He supposed he ought to phone Alex and tell him what had happened; yet he couldn't bring himself to do it. The problem, he felt, was his to solve. Alex, he knew, hadn't liked being moved into midfield at Turkdean even though it was an emergency measure. Alex believed United should have defended in depth and, possibly, he was right. Teams won matches, though, by playing attacking football: Damian would always support that idea. He didn't want to get into an argument with Alex, so perhaps it was best to continue to do things his way.

But if Neil and Stevie did leave, how was he going to replace them? United simply hadn't any spare players to call on and so his only hope was to find boys who weren't at present playing for other teams in the Redbourne Leagues. That wouldn't be easy – it might even be impossible – and certainly there was no chance at all of recruiting them before the next match. So he'd have to reshuffle the present pack to come up with a striker to play alongside Danny Clixby. Mentally, he went through the list.

There was, he decided, only one possibility: Matthew Morgan. The big centre-back had the height and the heading ability and he was pretty mobile. He might even be a *better* centre-forward than Neil, who regularly squandered chances that other strikers would put away with ease. On the debit side, Matt probably lacked a striker's instinct for being in the right place at the right time and he might not enjoy the idea of switching roles (though Damian suspected that every defender fancied himself as a goal scorer). Mark Scott could be drafted into defence to take Matt's place: but where would United find a player with Stevie's pace and flair on the ball? Damian's frown matched Neil's.

Then he remembered Warren and Ian. When might they be fit? Warren's injury wasn't as severe as Ian's and therefore he might be able to play quite soon, perhaps with a light plaster or some sort of bandaging over his wrist. It would be up to the referee, Damian knew, to decide whether someone was allowed to play with a protective covering on an arm or wrist. Really, he ought to ring Warren to see how he was getting on and to pass on news of team affairs.

He was just getting to his feet when his mother came in.

'Are you running a social club here, or something?' she inquired, standing just inside the doorway. 'I've never known so many visitors in one evening – for you.'

At that moment the doorbell rang. Damian was thoroughly amazed. 'You mean that's someone else for *me*? Who is it?'

Sue Tennant shrugged. 'Not sure, though I could make a guess about one of them. Saw them coming up the path when I glanced out of the bedroom window. You must be leading a secret life, Damian. I didn't know you'd got one girlfriend yet, let alone *two*. You must be a quick worker, my romantic young man!'

It was the first time she'd seen him blush in ages.

'Girls? G-girls?' he stammered. 'Can't be for *me*, Mum. Must be a mistake – wrong house.'

But it wasn't. In spite of her leg injury, which wasn't healing as fast as she'd hoped, it was Mrs Tennant who had to answer the door again and then usher the two girls into the sitting room.

'Oh, Elinor,' said Damian, recognising the girl who'd travelled with them to the Turkdean game. He should have guessed it would be her; after all, she'd declared a strong interest in soccer.

'Hi, Damian,' the slim girl with the rather businesslike spectacles greeted him, secretly delighted that he'd remembered her name. 'This is my best friend, Hayley – Hayley Marsh,' she added, introducing her companion whose mass of curly black hair and wide-mouthed grin would win her appreciative looks everywhere.

'I'll resume my role as café waitress at once,' announced Mrs Tennant, trying not to smile at the expression on her only son's face. 'I presume you young ladies would care for a drink and some biscuits?'

'Terrific!' was Elinor's enthusiastic reply. 'Thanks, Mrs Tennant.'

Then she turned her attention to Damian. 'Listen, I'm really sorry that United are having such a rotten time. You were *really* unlucky at Turkdean. You played some brilliant stuff to start with. I was most impressed. United have got some clever players. How's the boy who broke his arm? Ian, is that his name? The goal scorer.'

'Er, yes. Well, he's, er, getting along fine. But he'll be out of action for a bit, naturally.' By now Damian had worked out exactly what the girls wanted. But how would his team-mates react to the idea of playing alongside girls? And how was he going to find out if Elinor and Hayley were any good as footballers? He supposed, though, he could organize some sort of trial. After all, United did need new players.

'Oh, sorry about that,' responded Elinor, sounding genuinely sympathetic. 'So you're going to be short of a player, aren't you? Two, really, because somebody told me that Warren Snowball broke an arm, too. So United are really struggling with injuries as well as the bad luck?'

'It was Icy's wrist, actually,' Damian corrected her. 'Icy's what we call him, you know. But, yeah, we are struggling so I suppose you fancy a game for us, don't you? Well, what're your best skills? I mean, are you a striker or a defender? I would've thought – '

'*Play* for you?' Elinor cut in, her eyes widening enormously behind the glass lenses. 'I'm not a *player* – and neither is Hayley. OK, we kick a ball about a bit for fun but that's all it is. We know we're not, well, the right sort of shape for the real thing. No, Damian, honestly, we didn't think you'd want us in your team, however *desperate* you are! But you thought, well, what a fantastic *dream*, don't you think, Hayley?'

Hayley's eyes, too, were registering amazement and amusement as she nodded frantically. 'My brother'll die when I tell him about this,' she exploded. 'The idea of me hitting a thunderbolt into the net from about a hundred metres will just about bury him. Just hope he doesn't spread it around all the City players as a big joke. I mean, I like most of them and I don't want them thinking I'm trying to, well, muscle in on their game!'

Suddenly, as if she'd been struck by the most

hilarious happening imaginable, she collapsed backwards on to the sofa and continued to laugh delightedly from where she was lying. Elinor, too, was laughing but she at least remained on her feet. Then Mrs Tennant walked in with another laden tray.

'Well, I'm glad to hear there's something to laugh at at last,' she announced, placing the tray on the coffee table. 'There's been enough misery in this house lately to last a lifetime. So what's so funny?'

'Just a minute, Mum,' requested Damian, who'd suddenly seen an unexpected connection. 'Hayley, your brother's not *Darren* Marsh, is he, the City midfield player?'

'Well, of course! Who did you think he was? He's the only brother I've got, worse luck – or do I mean good luck?' Because she was still in the grip of some inner comedy it wasn't clear what she meant.

'How was I to know?' Damian asked exasperatedly. 'I didn't know he had a sister and, anyway, Elinor never mentioned you before – or him. But, well, you *must* be lucky. Fancy living in the same house as one of Redbourne City's star players!'

He shook his head in disbelief that anyone could *wonder* whether that *wasn't* the greatest good fortune. Think of the tips on how to improve your skills – the chance of free tickets for top matches – opportunities to meet other famous players . . . the list was practically endless. Then, as the girls sat down in a perfectly normal manner to eat and drink after rapidly recovering their composure, he remembered that he still hadn't found out *why* they were visiting him.

'So what've you come to see me for if you don't want to play for United?' he inquired.

Tactfully, Sue Tennant withdrew from the room before the girls could reply.

'Well, we felt United could do with cheering up so we're volunteering to be your cheerleaders,' Elinor replied calmly. 'We'll support you at every match and get spectators to cheer you on, too. We'll be really good at it, I promise.'

For a moment or two, Damian didn't know what to say. It was such an astonishing suggestion. He'd seen cheerleaders at American football games on TV but it hadn't occurred to him that they could be just as much an attraction at a British soccer match. Sometimes people dressed up as bears or pandas or rabbits or other creatures and paraded round the ground at half-time to raise money for charities; but, again, that was usually only at big league or cup matches.

'Would you – well – dress up in glittery gear and, er, short skirts? Oh, and do dancing to music? That sort of thing? Just the two of you?'

'Of course! We'd do it *properly*,' Elinor said positively. 'Oh, and it wouldn't be just us, we'd hope to get some other girls, friends of ours. There's Tanya Flockton and Jessica Kay for a start – I'm sure they'd *love* to be part of the team. Agreed, Hayley?'

Damian took a long sip at his Coke and then crunched a biscuit while he thought how to reply. He really couldn't see anything against the idea; it might appeal to some of the players who were already taking more than a passing interest in the subject of girlfriends. It was perfectly true that Darton United could do with some support, *any* support, really. Some really loud cheering, and possibly their name being chanted, at all these away matches would surely give a boost to the players.

'Well, I can't see anything *against* it,' he replied. Then, realising that was a rather lukewarm reaction he added: 'Actually, I think it would be a really good thing. Thanks for the, er, offer, Elinor – oh, and you, too, Hayley. Listen, will you be telling your brother about us? I mean, he may already have heard of us through Bryn Marsden, who used to be our president and coach.'

'Oh, definitely! We're good mates, really, even though we do scrap a bit sometimes. As you know, City are struggling at the moment in Div Two so Darren'll sympathise with another team that's having a bad time. Might even get him to come and watch a game one Sunday. You never know!'

'Well, that'd be great,' Damian enthused, already looking ahead to the possibility of one day soon inviting Darren Marsh to be their new coach. Things seemed to be looking up at last for United.

'We're going to have to scoot off now,' Elinor announced after emptying her glass of fizzy orange juice. 'Must see if we can round up some other girls to join our team. And we've also got to design a proper costume – in green and yellow to match United's colours. Good job my mum has a friend who runs a boutique and is really sharp with the old needlework! See you at Mortsea, Damian – oh, before, really, because Mum's promised to give you a lift again – and Neil – and Hayley – and – well, don't know yet but I know there'll be others. Thanks for the snack. Terrific!'

They departed at speed, which caused Sue Tennant's eyebrows to shoot up, but Damian wasn't in the mood for one of his mother's witticisms. The mention of Neil Dallimore had reminded him of a problem: and this time it was one he ought to discuss with Alex. But as he lifted the receiver and started to punch out the number buttons he was thinking that he also had some good news for his vice-captain, the first for a long time.

SIX

The Cheer Girls

Because there was likely to be nowhere at the Mortsea ground for them to change in, the Cheer Girls, as they were calling themselves, travelled in their costumes with rugs over their knees to keep themselves warm on a distinctly chilly autumn morning. So the brevity of their yellow skirts as they hurried over to the touchline to begin their warm-up routine took most of the players and spectators by surprise.

'Hey, look at that one, the one with the blonde hair going bananas with those knees-up jumps!' exclaimed Haji, who normally didn't express excitement about anything. 'She looks really great! I must find out her name. Maybe she lives near me!'

Damian, who had been watching Hayley with equally avid interest, just nodded. He loved the way her mane of black hair bounced up and down: and she moved beautifully. Then he realised he should be concentrating on team matters at this point with the game against Mortsea Gulls due to begin in less than ten minutes.

'How's your knee, Haji, the one you got a knock on against Turkdean?'

'Oh, fine now, thanks,' the goalie answered, not even leaning down to stroke the recently painful area. Yet, earlier in the week, he'd admitted he might not be fit enough to play today. 'Forgotten all about it, skipper.'

The biggest surprise of the day, though, apart from the appearance of United's new official cheerleaders, was the return to the team of Warren Snowball. Of course, his injured wrist was in a protective sleeve but the local referee raised no objection to his playing in it.

'I don't mind playing up front, either, if you want me to,' Icy told Damian when giving him the news about his availability. 'I've been thinking about the team's needs and my own game, of course. And I think I could do more around the box if you wanted me to.'

'Great, just what we need!' Damian replied delightedly. 'I'm moving Matt Morgan, too, into the forwards, so you and he can work up a new striking partnership. That'll teach Dalli-a-lot not to mess us about.'

As Damian had predicted, the two rebels, Neil and Stevie, hadn't been allowed to sign for another team at this stage of the season. Therefore they'd declared they were ready to resume playing for United (Damian doubted whether they'd really wanted to leave in the first place). However, he and Alex agreed the pair ought to be punished in some way for their lack of loyalty; so they'd been relegated to the role of substitutes for the current game. Matt, when he'd heard that Neil might be leaving, had seized his own opportunity to tell Damian he'd be willing to have a go as centre-forward, and Damian accepted the offer. Mark Scott, who'd been working hard in training sessions, was drafted into the defence in Matt's place. The captain regretted the loss of Stevie's pace on the wing but he felt that Warren's return, with all the skills he possessed, more than made up for it; in any case, United had the option of bringing Stevie on later in the game if a replacement was needed for anyone.

Because it was at the seaside and there were dunes on the other side of a boundary wall, the pitch had been well used during the summer; bare patches had been covered with sand following recent heavy rains and such conditions were bound to favour the Gulls.

Although it was hard to view it as such in the circumstances, this was actually a 'home' fixture for Darton; thus it was doubly important that they secured three points from the match. For once they'd brought a good contingent of supporters with them, including the parents of several of the cheerleaders who had also acted as chauffeurs to various members of the team. Damian was heartened by seeing so many people sporting green and yellow favours and applauding the players as they ran on to the pitch between two lines of the colourful Cheer Girls.

Dancing energetically, with a high-stepping

action, and flourishing huge green and yellow pompoms (which were attached by cords to the wrists so they couldn't be dropped), Elinor and Hayley and their four companions broke into a well-rehearsed chant the moment their team lined up for the kick-off.

'Watch Darton United
Go for goal, go for goal, go for GOALS
And Go for Growth
WATCH Darton UNI-TED!'

The players were so entranced they almost forgot to kick-off: either that or they didn't heed the referee's whistle. The Gulls were as white as their namesakes with only a red trim on their short-sleeved shirts. Compared to Darton and their fervent supporters they were truly colourless. They also seemed mesmerised by the girls and it was occurring to some of their players that a team bringing its own fan club and cheerleaders must be good. Though they weren't aware of it, United had already gained a notable psychological advantage over the opposition. Even Mortsea's own supporters found it hard to take their eyes off the girls and their distinctive attire.

Once again, United made a brilliant start. As if inspired by his return to the team as well as by the energy of the Cheer Girls, Warren Snowball seized control from the moment he first touched the ball. Collecting a sharply angled pass from Damian, he set off on a mazy run, fending off tackles both fierce and half hearted. With a neat change of pace he cut past a hesitant defender on the edge of the box, spun round in practically 360 degrees, spotted Matt Morgan rushing in – and delivered the perfect cross.

All Matt really had to do was to head it strongly towards his chosen target, the huge space to the right of the unmoving goalkeeper. Heading was the big defender's speciality and he wasn't going to lose the knack now he'd been converted into a centre-forward. With one flick of his neck, he buried the ball high in the net. For a boy who so desperately wanted to be recognised as a goal scorer, it was the dream start.

'Oh, terrific!' Damian exclaimed, unwittingly echoing Elinor's favourite expression. He raced across to congratulate both Matt and Warren, though he remembered to warn his players not to overdo it. 'Don't forget what happened to Ian Venn,' he added.

The caution was hardly necessary: they could all plainly see the medical sleeve on Warren's arm. Warren himself looked thrilled, as he deserved to do; his father was clapping on the touchline, his hands high above his head. He wasn't the only one who realised they'd just witnessed a goal created by a player of rare skills, a player who needed only the merest element of luck in life to ensure he had a great future in the game of soccer.

Naturally, the Cheer Girls were ecstatic. After another chorus of their own United song, they switched to the totaly unoriginal: 'There's only one Warren Snowball, one Warren Snowball, there's only . . .' It went on a bit but then, the girls were really enjoying themselves, fully believing that the goal was due at least in part to their own presence as supporters.

One of the Mortsea spectators seemed to be shooting an entire reel of film of the celebrating girls. He was a professional photographer and present mainly because his own son was one of the Gulls' back four. But, of course, he had an eye for a good shot (on film) and knew where to sell such a picture.

Damian's mind was now entirely on the game, which was why he was completely unaware of Elinor's appreciative glances in his direction whether or not he had the ball. If United managed to establish a good lead again he wouldn't make the mistake he had done against Turkdean; this time Darton would hold on to what they'd secured. He and Alex had discussed tactics and strategy in great detail in the past week and they were united in thought as well as in deed.

Mortsea were quite a useful side with some normally composed defenders. Their lapse in the opening moments of the game wasn't going to be repeated if they and their coach could do anything about it – and he was already shouting instructions from the touchline about new formations. Somebody was detailed to mark the leggy striker (as the coach referred to Warren) out of the game.

That was easier to imagine than to accomplish, as the coach quickly discovered. Icy had the temperament to go with his close control of the ball, so all efforts to dispossess him failed – when they were legitimate. And when they were illegal and the referee saw them United were awarded beneficial free kicks. It was from one of those, just outside the penalty area, that Darton contrived the opening to score their next goal.

Warren made a dummy run at the ball, Damian hit it with his left foot, swinging it to the far end of the defensive wall, Danny Clixby, well positioned for heading it into the middle, did just that, Matt stabbed at it instinctively. Somehow the ball squirmed through the goalie's hands as he bent down to grasp it . . . and rolled into the net. It was

a dreadfully unlucky goal for the Gulls but even Germany's top keeper had made mistakes in international matches in his time and presented opponents with unexpected gifts. Mortsea's goalie consoled himself with that thought as he retrieved the ball and punted it back to the middle, though he didn't suppose their coach would see it in those terms.

Matt really couldn't believe his luck. Fifteen minutes was all he'd played as a striker and already he'd scored twice: because, of course, he could justifiably claim that the second goal was his even though the goalie should have prevented it. He risked a look at Neil Dallimore on the touchline: and Dalli-a-lot predictably looked glum.

The Cheer Girls, naturally, were happier than ever. They had a new song (lyrics by Tanya Flockton):

> 'We're going top,
> We're going top
> We ARE going
> RIGHT to the TOP!'

Alex grinned at Damian as they lined up for the Gulls to kick off again: 'Could be right, too.'

Damian shook his head. 'Long way to go yet. Let's just make sure we win this one. Top managers always say they take each match as it comes.'

Mortsea's coach was looking mortified. From what he'd heard from friends in charge of Sunday League sides, Darton United had lost their way; the loss of their ground had upset them so much they were losing out in other directions, too. Well, to his eyes that didn't look true at all. *This* team was playing with verve and confidence and an abundance of skill. They couldn't have discovered all that in the space of a couple of matches. And teams that were on their way down didn't attract such noisy and attractive supporters as they'd brought with them. For the Gulls, this was listed as an away fixture and the coach had been certain they'd swoop off with three points. He swallowed hard: the way things were going, they could suffer their biggest defeat of the season and it would be on their own pitch.

As it turned out, though, their defence played with greater resolution from then on and the goalkeeper recovered his handling skills. So United, in spite of mounting innumerable attacks, didn't manage to score again before half-time. Still, the Gulls couldn't get the ball in the net, either.

During the interval the United players relaxed with fruit drinks and glucose sweets provided by enthusiastic parents; the Cheer Girls shared the refreshments but, uncertain whether the boys wanted to talk to them at this time for tactical discussions, they merely hovered on the edge of the group beside the pitch. Damian's message to his team was brief: 'We mustn't let this one slip. So we've got to tackle like tigers to keep possession – and hit 'em again as soon as we get the chance. I don't reckon much to their goalie so we must fire in shots from *any* distance whenever

101

anybody gets in shooting range.'

Somehow, the Mortsea coach managed to stoke up his team with new determination to get something out of the match. So, as everyone expected, they started the second half with a series of all-out attacks. United's defence, though, never wavered; marshalled by Alex, who was in superb form, they repelled every onslaught so that Hajinder really had very little to do. Yet, when United turned defence into offence, they didn't make the progress they hoped for, not least because Warren was being shackled by a man-to-man marker who was as tenacious as a greyhound pursuing a hare. In fact, the sandy surface seemed to be sapping Icy's stamina (his injury having taken more out of him than anyone suspected).

Damian knew he should be satisfied with a two-goal lead, especially as he was increasingly confident the Gulls wouldn't score. All the same, a third goal would *surely* clinch the game for United. So, after Warren had limped away from a crunching tackle that brought the defender a deserved booking, Damian raced across to thank him for his contribution and said: 'But I think you need a rest now. So I'm bringing on Stevie as your sub. If he stays on the wing a bit he can pull their defence out of position.'

It worked. Within five minutes of coming on to the pitch Stevie, thrilled to be back in action, took the ball almost to the corner flag, magnetizing one of the Mortsea defenders as he did so. Then, beating him in a tight turn, Stevie headed for the box before hitting his cross towards the far post where Matt had positioned himself. As Matt went up for the header he heard Damian's yell: 'I'm here!' Coolly and neatly, Matt headed the ball back towards the in-rushing Damian instead of trying to score himself. And Damian easily side-footed it into the net through the unprotected area beside the upright.

After that, the Gulls simply flopped. Stevie should have added a fourth goal but delayed his shot too long when he had only the goalie to beat. But 3–0 was a very satisfying scoreline.

With another rousing rendition of the new United anthem, 'We're going top,' the Cheer Girls formed twin lines again as their triumphant team left the pitch. Elinor gave Damian a hug. She would have liked it to be a kiss but it might be too soon for that, she decided. She'd also noted the glances he'd been bestowing on Hayley, though she hoped that was simply because Hayley was Darren Marsh's sister.

Elinor remarked, 'I liked the substitution, Damian. Great timing! It's just what I'd've done if I'd been skipper.'

'You know,' Alex beamed, 'I think our luck could've changed at last.'

Neil heard that but didn't seem convinced. 'Better keep our fingers crossed, then, that it stays that way,' he muttered. But no one was listening to him.

SEVEN

In the News

Carefully, Hayley Marsh slid the local free newspaper across the dining table to a position where her brother's eyes simply couldn't miss the photograph across four columns at the top of the page. Darren was casually thumbing through a number of fan letters he'd brought home from Redbourne City Football Club the previous evening. He was wondering how many he could afford to ignore, though he supposed he should answer a few to clear his conscience. Trouble was, he just *hated* writing letters; he never had any idea what to say.

Hayley's unaccustomed silence, followed by the movement of the paper, made Darren look up: and he saw the picture. For several moments, deliberately extended to annoy Hayley who was obviously anxious for a reaction, he just studied it through narrowed eyes.

'Oh, come on, Daz, what d'you think?' she burst out as her patience dissolved. 'Great, isn't it? Don't you think all the girls look really terrific in that outfit? I mean, wouldn't you like to see us cheering *your* team like that?'

Darren grinned. 'Oh, I think you all look a bit too young for the City lads! I mean, if you were five or six years *older*, well – '

'Daz, be *serious*. Listen, the players thought we were great because they had a terrific win away from home. Oh, no, not really – I mean they were *supposed* to be at home but because they haven't got a pitch of their own now they were actually playing their home match away . . . er, if you see what I mean.'

'Not really, no. So you'd better explain. For once, I think I'd rather listen to you, Hey-Hey, than answer these gushy letters. Go on.'

So she did, telling him in some detail about Darton United, their plight and their progress and their promotion hopes and how she and Elinor and several of their friends were now United's official Cheer Girls.

'It was Elinor who got the idea, and she roped me in,' Hayley admitted. 'She really fancies Damian, I think, though she won't *confess* that. I don't blame her, he is an attractive boy, though he's not very tall. Still . . . He's a good captain, no doubt about it. I'm sure he'll lead them to the top. All the team needs is a bit of luck – now they've got us!'

Darren pushed the paper aside and gave an exaggerated sigh. 'Luck! I think that's what City are going to need when we play Cologne in the Cup next week. On the plus side, though, it'll be a new experience to visit Germany – new for most of the lads as well as for me. Hope the hospitality's good. We may need all the consolation we can find!'

'Wish I was going with you,' his sister remarked wistfully and predictably. 'Then I'd miss all those boring science lessons and maths and – '

'But you'd also miss doing all that spectacular dancing and cheering, to say nothing of, what's his name, yes, *Damian* and Darton United,' cut in Darren, his grin wider still. 'That'd be a terrible loss, wouldn't it?'

'Well, at least you've remembered the names,' Hayley murmured as her brother swept up his correspondence and headed for his own room.

The item appeared in every national newspaper, most local papers and even on television's teletext service. The wording hardly varied at all wherever it was printed. It read:

> Redbourne City, the Second Division side, have won the Performance of the Week Award for their remarkable 1–0 victory over Cologne in the Top City Trophy. The Award from the sponsors, which consists of a set of tracksuits and training equipment for a local boys' team of the winner's choice, has been donated to Darton United, a Sunday League side.

Damian shook his head repeatedly, as if half dazed. 'I still don't really believe it,' he kept saying to anyone who would listen. And, at the presentation ceremony in the Players' Lounge at the City Ground, there were lots of people who were listening to almost everything that was being said.

Only a couple of the City players were present but one of them was Darren Marsh who, it turned out, had recommended United for the Award because he remembered Hayley's remarks about the team after she'd become one of their Cheer Girls. And Darren had been allowed to make the choice because he'd scored the goal that overcame Cologne – and goals from him were rare.

For the benefit of a press photographer, the boys dutifully put on their magenta and white tracksuits and held up the half dozen match balls that were included in the Award. Temporarily the tracksuits covered up their green shirts bearing the logo and wording of their own sponsors but everybody assured them that wouldn't matter just for once. After all, their sponsors would probably get additional publicity in future when United attracted greater support as a result of their new fame.

A reporter from the same newspaper asked Damian whether he could possibly imagine a better gift than the one the team had just received. He expected a conventional 'Oh no!' as an answer.

'Well, there is one thing,' replied Damian matter-of-factly. 'I just wish we'd been given a new pitch instead so we could really play our home games at home.'

'What d'you mean?' the reporter asked. So Damian told him.

One day in the near future, the reporter would go to work for one of Britain's top daily newspapers because he was bright and talented and very determined to get what he wanted out of life. Best of all, he could recognise a good story the moment he got a hint of it. So he asked Damian to tell him more, to tell him everything he needed to know to write a much better story than anything he'd expected to get from this very ordinary presentation.

After the reporter had thanked him, pocketed his tape recorder and moved away to confer with his photographer, Damian noticed that no one was talking to Darren Marsh at that moment. That seemed to be a lucky chance, so he seized it.

'Thanks again, Darren, for recommending us for this Award,' he said earnestly. 'We're really, well, *chuffed* to get it. It's great.'

'Glad to be of help,' the City midfielder told him warmly. 'Hey-Hey – Hayley, I mean – well, she thinks a lot of you – all your team, I mean. She's actually a fair player herself, when I let her have a kick!'

Hayley wasn't really the person he wanted to talk about, so Damian just nodded, waiting for an opening. Then, when Darren glanced at his wristwatch, he knew he must strike now.

'I was wondering – the team were wondering – well, whether you'd be willing to coach us, Darren. You know Bryn Marsden used to be our coach before he went to Charlton? Well, I think we really need somebody to take his place. Then, well, we might really go places.'

Darren didn't know what to say or, rather, how to say what was really in his mind. He didn't want to disappoint this enthusiastic young footballer who, he suspected, possessed some of his own qualities and determination to get to the top in soccer. On the other hand, Darren was basically rather lazy off the pitch and he didn't want to give up his precious free time.

'Er, well, I can't promise anything at the moment, Damian. I'm really a bit busy, you see,' he answered until, suddenly, a brilliant idea came to him. 'Tell you what, though, if you win your League this season I'll definitely coach you from then on. How about that?'

'Great!' exclaimed Damian, having really got as much as he'd hoped for. 'So now United have got *another* good reason for getting to the top. Thanks, Darren. Hayley'll let you know how we're getting on, won't she?'

Darren grinned. 'No doubt about that at all!'

Jack Donnen put aside the newspaper he'd been devouring, page by page, leaned back in his black leather chief executive's chair, closed his eyes and directed his mind to some of the most joyous moments of his childhood. When he was Damian Tennant's age Mr Donnen's happiest times were spent on a football pitch with his mates; there he could forget about the miseries of life with his grandparents who could never understand what really mattered to him in life. They thought they were doing him a favour just by giving him a home after his parents were killed in a plane crash. They thought that was more than enough and he ought to be thoroughly grateful. To Jack, their home would never be his home as long as he lived.

Football was something he'd had to sacrifice after starting his own business as a teenager, buying and selling what other people regarded as junk; making money was exciting and money gave him the independence he craved. Sometimes he thought wistfully that it was a pity he gave up the game because, really, he was good at it and might have made it his career.

Still, he reflected, even if he'd played for Arsenal or Man United he'd never have earned the millions that JayDee Packaging, the company he'd created, had brought him. Nowadays, he was too busy to play soccer even for fun with his own children, but the game still captivated him.

He leaned forward and pressed a switch on the console on his desk. His personal assistant answered instantaneously. 'Yes, Jay Dee?'

'James, remember when we took over The Handy Boxes Company last year? We sold off some land but we kept their sports complex in case we got planning permission for further development. Well, nobody uses it on Sundays, do they? To play any sports, I mean.'

'I don't think so, Jay Dee, but I'll check on it.'

'Good, because I've been reading about a boys'

Sunday League team that's got a bit of a problem. And I've had an idea . . .'

Whenever the Boss said he had an idea his personal assistant noted all the details immediately. And then acted on them with the same speed.

EIGHT

Home Team

'I don't believe this,' Damian murmured. 'I just don't.'

He knew he'd said that before, said it several times, but he still couldn't stop himself from saying it yet again. For it was true: it was almost impossible to believe that their luck could have switched so dramatically from bad to good in so short a time.

'Well, this really proves it,' Alex Anson pointed out, patting the embossed words on the pale green door that led to the changing room. They read: Home Team. 'And the place is all ours, every Sunday we need it. Fantastic but true!'

'Can't wait to try out the showers after the match,' exclaimed Danny Clixby, tentatively trying one of the shining taps and then hastily stepping back when hot water jetted down on him. 'Hey, look at the steam already! D'you think we should have showers now and then we'll be able to clean up the opposition? We'll wash Drilby Firebirds down the plughole, put their flames out for ever!'

It was hardly a good joke, it was hardly a joke at

all, but because they were in such high spirits most of the Darton United players shared in the laughter. Their first viewing of the JayDee Packaging Sports Ground was even more rewarding than they'd imagined in their most optimistic moments. None of them had expected there to be hot showers that worked and cushioned seats on the dressing-room benches and lockers, complete with keys, for their clothes. The pitch itself, which they'd inspected in a state of some awe, was impeccably marked out on practically perfect grass and so smooth it wouldn't disturb a spirit level. Naturally, the goal posts had been freshly painted and the nets were brand new.

'Listen, the one thing we've got to make sure we do is to thank Mr Donnen when we get out there just before the kick-off,' Damian told them earnestly as they settled down and started to change out of their clothes. 'I want everybody to say it personally, not just me – and give him a handshake, OK? Businessmen are always shaking hands with each other, like politicians.'

'I thought you told us, after you met him, that he said the best way of thanking him was to win all our home matches?' Alex remarked.

Damian, pulling on his yellow shorts, nodded. 'Right, but that doesn't mean we shouldn't do it again, each of us. Anyway, he said the press photographers would be here so I expect they'll want pictures of us all together – you know, Mr Donnen in the middle with the team grouped round him. Good publicity for us again, you know.'

'And for Jack Donnen and for JayDee Packaging or whatever it's called,' observed Hajinder, who'd already decided he was going to be a successful businessman as well as an international goalkeeper.

'Fair enough, he deserves it,' said Stevie Pailthorp, who was always in a good mood these days now that he'd been restored to the team from the start of each game. 'You know what? I think we should have a whip-round and buy him a present for what he's done for us. How about a box of cigars? That's what tycoons smoke, isn't it? And the paper's always calling him a tycoon. Nice word, that.'

'Good thinking,' Damian agreed. 'But we don't need a whip-round. We've got cash in our Save United Fund, remember. My car-cleaning round, Merch's recycled cans, Alex's Mum's veggie goodies that we sold – I mean, we've hardly dipped into the petrol money, either. And now we'll not need that as we can get to this ground on our own.'

'Right, then, I vote we dig into our fund and give Mr Donnen a present,' Alex said purposefully. He'd begun to feel lately that he wasn't contributing enough to team matters off the field. 'All agreed?'

He glanced round and saw that everyone, including the skipper, of course, was nodding approval. 'Right, good. And I'll be responsible for getting the gift for Damian to present to him before our next home match. We could also invite him to be our president. I'm sure he'd want to, er, continue to help us in all sorts of ways.'

'Good thinking,' Damian said again. 'But today

we've got to show him we're *worth* supporting. So we've got to WIN. Nothing else will do. So let's get out there, men, and warm up for the battle. We're going to shoot these Firebirds down, bang, bang!'

On that exultant note he led the team out of the changing room, patting the green door on the way for luck, and on to the wide expanse of emerald turf in front of the twin soccer pitches. Mr Donnen, wearing a white raincoat with a fur-trimmed collar, was waiting to greet them, predictably his hand already extended to shake the captain's. And two photographers were present to take the sort of pictures they liked when a local celebrity was involved.

Naturally, the team's Cheer Girls were delighted to be included, too. Following the publicity they received after the Mortsea game their numbers had increased and there were now ten of them. Of course, Elinor and Hayley were still the official leaders, Hayley's stature having improved immeasurably once it was realised that Darren Marsh was her brother and a declared Darton United supporter.

'Daz said to tell you he's thinking of the team this morning and keeping his fingers crossed that you'll have a terrific win,' Hayley relayed to Damian as they came close together for yet another photographic pose. Casually, or so it seemed, she slipped her arm round his waist; and Damian didn't attempt to disengage himself.

'Did he say anything about being our coach?' United's captain inquired.

'Not yet but don't worry, I'm working on it,'
replied the dark-haired girl, giving him a squeeze as
if to emphasise the point. 'Trust me.'

Elinor had heard and seen everything and it
wasn't easy to maintain a real smile for the benefit
of the cameraman. But she did it and thought about
the future; she guessed she'd just have to be patient.
In fact, sometimes to her parents' surprise, Elinor
was good at being patient.

The Drilby team, wearing black shorts and with
small gold flames embroidered on their crimson
shirts, stood and gazed in some astonishment at all
the fuss surrounding their opponents. Originally,
they'd believed this would be as good as a home
match to them. Now, however, they really were

away, playing at a venue they'd never seen before today. All the same, their coach had ordered them to treat it as a home match and attack from the outset. 'Let Darton do the worrying,' he repeated more than once.

The visitors couldn't help being impressed by the energy and the full-throated vocal support United were getting from their Cheer Girls. Because the girls had formed their usual tunnel Damian and his team felt it was only fair to run on to the pitch between the two lines: and that had the effect of enlivening their other supporters still further.

Because the match marked the reopening of the old Handy Boxes Sports Arena it had attracted a number of casual spectators, most of whom promptly decided to support the new 'home' side. Among United's own supporters was Ian Venn, who would soon be getting rid of the plaster on his arm. He'd decided it was going to be third time lucky for him with United and Damian had promised him a place in the squad as soon as Ian was fully fit again.

'Watch Darton United . . . Go for Goal, go for goal . . .' the girls chorused as soon as the match kicked off. But it wasn't United going for goal first: it was the Firebirds, blazing away immediately. And, to the home team's horror, they scored in only the third minute.

Drilby's opening raids all broke down, mainly because of over-eagerness on the part of their forwards, but Darton still couldn't get the ball into the opposite half of the pitch until Warren tried to send Stevie away down the right wing. Unhappily, it wasn't an accurate pass; the ball was intercepted by a red-shirted midfielder who immediately pumped it up the middle again; and once more a Drilby striker went in pursuit of it. Mark Scott, United's improving central defender, dashed across to be the first to reach it. He succeeded and then, because he was on his own on the edge of the box, he turned to pass the ball back to his goalkeeper and safety. But in his anxiety to do the right thing he under-hit the pass and the Drilby striker, still on the move, saw his chance.

Haji, seeing the danger a fraction later than he should have done, was slow to come out. In his despair he flung himself at the ball in an attempt to smother it. Nimbly, his opponent took the ball round the stricken keeper and joyfully slammed it into the net.

Damian swallowed his instant dismay. Was United's season going to turn sour again, after all? But the goal was due to a mistake, not bad luck. Human error: that's what it was. He raced across to Mark and Haji, who were still eyeing each other in a kind of disbelief.

'Look, forget it!' he told them as calmly as possible. 'OK, there was a mistake but don't *worry* about it. It was just one of those things. Keep playing your normal game, OK?'

They nodded, amazed that Damian hadn't blasted them for what they thought of as two dreadful errors. If the skipper could shrug them off, then so could they. There was still more than an hour of the game remaining to put things right. That was Jack Donnen's view, too. As a businessman, he was used to encountering obstacles when trying to set up a deal: but finding ways of overcoming them often brought out the best in the people on your team. So that early setback for United didn't cause him to raise so much as an eyebrow.

The Cheer Girls were the ones who were the most upset; they'd been shocked into complete silence. Hayley was the first to recover. After one glance at Damian's stricken expression she told them: 'Come on, this is when they *need* to hear us. Let's give 'em our loudest chorus. GO for goal, GO, GO, GO!'

It worked. The Firebirds expected United to hit back immediately but they didn't imagine the urgency would be sustained for so long or that their opponents would attack with such width. Warren Snowball drifted out to the left and when Danny supplied the sort of pass he wanted, Icy kept possession, deftly beating one opponent right on the touchline and then repeating the trick against the same player seconds later. Only when he'd attracted extra attention from baffled defenders did Icy release the ball – and then he swept it more than half-way across the pitch to Matt Morgan.

'Mine, Matthew!' Stevie Pailthorp yelled, cutting in from the opposite flank. With commendable quick thinking, Matt made no attempt to keep the ball: he simply flicked it sideways for Stevie to run on to and shoot. The shot was powerfully struck, too powerfully for the goalkeeper to hold although he got both hands to the ball. As it bounced away from him Matt, following up, planted it in the net with aplomb.

What chiefly delighted Damian about the equalizer was Stevie's confident call for the ball and Matt's immediate response. That was exactly the kind of link-up he'd been demanding in training sessions. Within two minutes, he and United had further cause for celebration. The Firebirds committed themselves to an all-out counter-attack but it broke down when Mark Scott made an interception and hoofed the ball to Damian.

With Drilby's midfielders having charged upfield to join their own attack United's skipper had no opponent within metres of him as he set off to run with the ball. His acceleration and body-swerve took him past the first challenger and, on the edge of the box, he actually nutmegged the lone defender. Sensibly, the goalkeeper came off his line, determined to prevent a goal this time. But his co-defenders had left him woefully exposed. Damian thought of taking the ball all the way into the net but, catching a glimpse of the electric Danny out of the corner of his eye, he called: 'Yours, Danny.' And slid the ball sideways. Danny had never been known to miss a completely open goal and he didn't spoil that record.

From then on, and for most of the rest of the match, United played some almost dream-like football on the flawless turf of their new home pitch.

Damian wasn't their only inspiration, though; Icy, revelling in his new roaming role, was in his finest form. Part of his confidence came from the fact that he knew Danny and Matt were the sort of strikers who could be relied on to convert the chances he created into goals.

In spite of being 1–3 down at half-time (United's third goal being scored by Matt with a header), Drilby began to play some attractive football, too, in the second half. So spectators, casual as well as committed, had plenty to applaud; and no one seemed more pleased with things than Jack Donnen, who was already wondering what else he could do to support this delightful team in the green shirts and yellow shorts.

The Cheer Girls were, of course, ecstatic as well as in excellent voice. All that the game lacked so far, as Elinor and Hayley saw it, was a goal from Damian. But he wasn't particularly interested in scoring himself and he was perfectly happy to set up United's fourth, a diving header from Matt.

That was the goal that caused the girls to switch to what they were now thinking of as their victory chorus.

> 'We're going top,
> We're going top
> We ARE going
> RIGHT to the TOP!'

Damian wasn't the only one present who believed that.

Also by Michael Hardcastle

THE TEAM THAT WOULDN'T GIVE IN

Ian, Damian and Alex have decided they can, and will, change their football team's luck. Darton United are at the bottom of the Redbourne Sunday Junior League. Though jinxed by a spell of accidents, the boys know that if they don't improve their game they will be out of the League for good. Together, the three friends bravely determine to lead their team on to success . . .

Michael Hardcastle

MASCOT

When Damian Tennant is chosen by his local Football League club to be their mascot, it's the happiest day of his life. But his selection causes jealousy among his team-mates and threatens his captaincy of Sunday League side Darton United. He must prove to them he's the leader they need – but how?

Michael Hardcastle

AWAY FROM HOME

Keith can't believe it when he's selected for the Town Boys' soccer squad. What's more, two of his Bank Vale United team-mates are chosen as well. Then they discover that some of their Sunday League rivals are also in the side . . .

The freedom of playing away from home provides plenty of excitement on and off the pitch.

Michael Hardcastle

FREE KICK

Oakland Rangers need a new captain. Six players think they're right for the job. How will they choose?

A Superstars Contest is the answer – a test of each player's all-round sporting ability. But in the end, everything hangs on footballing skill . . .

A Selected List of Fiction from Mammoth

While every effort is made to keep prices low, it is sometimes necessary to increase prices at short notice. Mandarin Paperbacks reserves the right to show new retail prices on covers which may differ from those previously advertised in the text or elsewhere.

The prices shown below were correct at the time of going to press.

☐	7497 0978 2	**Trial of Anna Cotman**	Vivien Alcock	£2.50
☐	7497 0712 7	**Under the Enchanter**	Nina Beachcroft	£2.50
☐	7497 0106 4	**Rescuing Gloria**	Gillian Cross	£2.50
☐	7497 0035 1	**The Animals of Farthing Wood**	Colin Dann	£3.50
☐	7497 0613 9	**The Cuckoo Plant**	Adam Ford	£3.50
☐	7497 0443 8	**Fast From the Gate**	Michael Hardcastle	£1.99
☐	7497 0136 6	**I Am David**	Anne Holm	£2.99
☐	7497 0295 8	**First Term**	Mary Hooper	£2.99
☐	7497 0033 5	**Lives of Christopher Chant**	Diana Wynne Jones	£2.99
☐	7497 0601 5	**The Revenge of Samuel Stokes**	Penelope Lively	£2.99
☐	7497 0344 X	**The Haunting**	Margaret Mahy	£2.99
☐	7497 0537 X	**Why The Whales Came**	Michael Morpurgo	£2.99
☐	7497 0831 X	**The Snow Spider**	Jenny Nimmo	£2.99
☐	7497 0992 8	**My Friend Flicka**	Mary O'Hara	£2.99
☐	7497 0525 6	**The Message**	Judith O'Neill	£2.99
☐	7497 0410 1	**Space Demons**	Gillian Rubinstein	£2.50
☐	7497 0151 X	**The Flawed Glass**	Ian Strachan	£2.99

All these books are available at your bookshop or newsagent, or can be ordered direct from the publisher. Just tick the titles you want and fill in the form below.

Mandarin Paperbacks, Cash Sales Department, PO Box 11, Falmouth, Cornwall TR10 9EN.

Please send cheque or postal order, no currency, for purchase price quoted and allow the following for postage and packing:

UK including BFPO — £1.00 for the first book, 50p for the second and 30p for each additional book ordered to a maximum charge of £3.00.

Overseas including Eire — £2 for the first book, £1.00 for the second and 50p for each additional book thereafter.

NAME (Block letters) ....

ADDRESS ....

....

☐ I enclose my remittance for ....

☐ I wish to pay by Access/Visa Card Number

Expiry Date